CW00811182

Readings from

James

J

trials ➕ faith ➕ riches ➕ prayer

Tim Shenton

© Day One Publications
Ryelands Road Leominster HR6 8NZ
email: sales@dayone.co.uk
www.dayone.co.uk

UK Tel: 01568 613 740
Fax: 01568 611 473

EuropeTel: ++ 44 1568 613 740

United States Tel: 706 554 5907
or Toll Free: 1-8-morebooks

Canada Tel: 519 763 0339

ISBN: 1 903087 61 9

Design Wild Associates Ltd   **Tel:** 0208 715 9224

To my two wonderful girls,
Abbie and Sarah

Contents

Introduction

After the stoning of Stephen in Acts 7, a great persecution broke out against the church and many of the believers had to flee from their homes. James, who was the brother of Jesus, is writing to these Christians 'scattered among the nations' to encourage them to draw near to God in their daily lives.

Practise what you preach

James wants them to practise what they preach. It is so important to 'live the talk', as I heard someone put it. Being a Christian is not just believing the right things, but it's living the right life. Now James is urging his Christian friends to live in a way that pleases God, and not to use persecution as an excuse for disobedience.

> ## Listen!
> ### Jesus must be number one in your life

In your daily life, resist temptation and obey God's Word, so that you can prove your faith by your deeds. Be careful not to show favouritism and set a guard over your mouth, for the words you say can deeply hurt others. Always submit to God and turn from your sins. And in all your troubles, be patient. At the right time God will deliver you. He is full of mercy and compassion, and will not let you suffer more than you are able to endure.

> ## The Bible says:
> Jesus said to his disciples, 'If anyone would come after me, he must deny himself and take up his cross and follow me.'
>
> ## Matthew 16:24

And always remember to pray and praise. If times are hard, cry out to God to give you the strength to keep going. If you are happy, praise him for his love and the gift of joy and peace.

The message of James

His message is this: Come what may, give your whole life to Jesus the whole of the time. Never turn your back on him even for a moment. When children at school say nasty things about you because of your faith, rejoice because God is making you stronger through the trials. When everything seems to go wrong, keep trusting in Jesus, because God has promised to give the crown of life to all who love him.

Stand up for Jesus

Simply put, that is the message of James. May the Lord bless you as you read and pray. May he encourage you to stand up for Christ in what you believe and in the way you live. If you are not a Christian, my prayer is that you will see how wonderful Jesus is and turn to him before you reach the end of this book.

1 'Consider it Pure Joy'

JAMES 1:1-8

'Consider it pure joy, my brothers, whenever you face trials of many kinds.'

Is James being serious? Are we really to consider 'trials of many kinds' pure joy? But trials and troubles upset us and hurt us. Sometimes they make us sad or angry. We don't get what we want, we feel pain, we stay awake at night worrying.

Are you being bullied?

Just imagine you are being bullied at school. Perhaps there is this one child who always picks on you. Whatever you do, he always makes some nasty comment and tries to get others to laugh at you. When you walk past him, he pinches you and whispers a nasty name into your ear. At break times he 'accidentally on purpose' knocks your biscuit on the ground and then stands on it. Or if you're playing football against him, he tries hard to hurt you in a tackle. How are you meant to react? What do you do?

Are you ill?

What's your attitude like when you're ill? Let's say you have to miss the school trip because you are ill in bed with the flu. Or you can't go on that amazing skiing holiday because you've broken your arm playing netball.

Ice-skating

I recently went ice-skating at our local rink and I was absolutely hopeless! I spent most of the time hanging on to the side for dear life. Some of the skaters were very good and whizzed past me so quickly. I think they were showing off a bit! There was one young man - he must have been about twenty-five - who was skating that day and I think he was almost as bad as me. The only difference was, he was holding a small child. As I slowly approached him, tiny step after tiny step, I saw him lose his balance. One leg went one way, the other leg went the other way. His free arm was searching desperately for something to hold onto as he started to turn round and round. He held on tightly to the child, until he completely lost his balance. He dropped the child, who banged his head on the ice and immediately started screaming. The man fell awkwardly on his knee and I think he broke it. He just lay on the ice, groaning in pain and unable to help his suffering child. Soon the St John's ambulance men came and helped him.

That man and his child went skating to have a fun afternoon, but it all went sadly wrong. I wonder how he reacted? If he was a Christian, did he count his troubles 'pure joy'?

How do you react? If you are being bullied at school, what is your response? If you have ever missed a dream holiday due to illness, what were your feelings?

Consider Jesus

Just consider Jesus for a moment. Peter tells us that when Jesus suffered, and he suffered much more than we will ever suffer, 'he committed no sin, and no deceit was found in his mouth'. When people

Whatever happens, fix your eyes on Jesus.

said nasty things about him, which was a form of adult bullying, he did not get them back and he made no threats. Of course, he could have destroyed them with the breath of his mouth, but instead he 'entrusted himself to him who judges justly'. (1 Peter 2:21-23). In Hebrews it says about Jesus that 'for the joy set before him he endured the cross, scorning its shame'. (Hebrews 12:2).

Pure joy? Yes!

So why should we count it 'pure joy' when we face trials of many kinds? Well, I could give you lots of reasons, but I will give you just three. When we experience troubles our faith, which is worth more than

> In times of trouble, run to Jesus as fast as you can. Remember, he is only a prayer away.

gold, is being tested and proved genuine. Genuine faith results in praise to God, and glory and honour for the believer when Jesus returns. I expect you value gold, which perishes. Then how much more should you value true faith, which will lead you into a heavenly inheritance, which can never perish, spoil or even fade.

Another reason is that when we are going through difficulties, we are much more likely to run to Jesus for help. Just as a toddler runs to her mum when she falls over and grazes her knee, so every true Christian will run to Jesus when he is afraid or in danger. Remember the disciples in the storm. They were afraid that they were going to drown so they ran to Jesus who was asleep in the boat, woke him up and cried out, 'Lord, save us!' If there had been no storm, they would have left Jesus sleeping. When our lives are

shaken, we will shelter under the shadow of his wing.

The last reason I shall give is that times of trial give God the opportunity to show his love and power. If the disciples had not been terrified by the storm, they would not have woken up their Saviour, nor experienced one of his greatest miracles. They were so amazed at the power of Jesus that they said to one another, 'What kind of man is this? Even the winds and the waves obey him!' (Matthew 8:27). When we are frightened and in trouble, we cry out to Jesus and he gives us a fresh taste of his love and power.

Thank God for trials

So never despise times of trouble. Thank God for them. Submit to his will. Obey him all the more and pray that you will never just be a 'fair-weather believer'. Don't feel sorry for yourself, but think about

all the blessings that come from trials, and rejoice in our wonderful Saviour, who never changes.

Think about Habakkuk

I shall end by quoting from Habakkuk, for whom farming and agriculture were so important. Consider his attitude and imitate it. 'Though the fig-tree does not bud and there are no grapes on the vines, though the olive crop fails and the fields produce no food, though there are no sheep in the pen and no cattle in the stalls, yet I will rejoice in the Lord, I will be joyful in God my Saviour.' (Habakkuk 3:17-18).

> **Memory Verse**
> 'If you suffer as a Christian, do not be ashamed, but praise God that you bear that name.'
>
> **1 Peter 4:16.**

Time to think

1 Are you experiencing any trials at the moment?

2 If you are, how have you been responding to them?

3 What was one of the things Jesus said to his persecutors when he was being crucified?

Time to pray

1 **Ask God to forgive you for not trusting him with your whole heart.**

2 **Ask God to help you to run to him in times of difficulty.**

3 **Pray for someone you know who is finding life tough.**

2 Never Give Up

JAMES 1:1-8

'Consider it pure joy, my brothers, whenever you face trials of many kinds, because you know that the testing of your faith develops perseverance.'

A testing time

The first thing I must mention is that when our faith is being tested it is not easy. Remember it is a test. If you have ever taken an important examination, then you'll know it is a 'testing' time. You have many years of instruction and information to be given to you by your teachers, you have notes to write and learn, research and course work, and then the day of the final exam. You might have stayed up late for many nights revising and preparing, you may feel nervous before the exam, and terrified of the result! All in all, it was not a pleasant experience and one I'm sure you could have done without, and yet hopefully your grade was good and you could go on to higher and better things.

A roller coaster?

If we return to the disciples in the storm on the Sea of Galilee, it was not something they enjoyed. They were not saying to each other, 'Oh, this is great fun! A bit like a roller coaster! I wish we could experience this every day.' No, of course not! They were afraid, thinking they

'Without warning, a furious storm came up on the lake, so that the waves swept over the boat. But Jesus was sleeping. The disciples went and woke him, saying, "Lord, save us! We're going to drown."'

Matthew 8:24-25

were going to drown. They were fighting hard in order to save their lives. And finally, as a last resort it seems, they cried out to Jesus.

Doubts

When our faith is tested it is a time of trial. Maybe we have really prayed about something and believed God was going to answer us, but nothing has happened. It is a test of faith, isn't it? We begin to doubt God. We say to ourselves, 'Has God really heard my prayer? Is he going to answer? Does he care? Is he interested?' In other

words, we struggle with doubts. There is nothing unusual about that. Everyone goes through these times of wondering where God is and whether or not he has heard our cry.

The example of a snail

As we've seen from our reading the testing of our faith 'develops perseverance', that is, it gives us the ability to keep going through thick and thin. I love the saying: 'Even the snail, by perseverance, reached Noah's ark.' Yes, that little creature must have had all sorts of problems on the way - climbing over twigs and stones and leaves, hiding from hungry birds, searching for food, finding the right direction and so on. And it must have taken years. But it kept going, and eventually reached the ark of salvation and was rescued from the flood.

Turn to Jesus

Now I know that was a silly example, but it makes the point. We must press on during times of trial. Never give up. Hold on to Jesus with all your might. Fix your

P8

Answer this question:

If you don't turn to Jesus in times of trouble, to whom do you turn?

eyes on him. Trust him and serve him come what may. He will see you through. He will keep you on that narrow road that leads to eternal life. Soon the ark of salvation will be in sight and you will be rescued from the wrath to come. This is why the testing of our faith develops perseverance,

because it teaches us to turn to Jesus and to draw all our strength from him so we can make it to the end. And what a glorious end we have in view, to be in heaven forever with our Saviour Jesus!

Mountain climbing

Last year my family and I went on a camping holiday to Austria. One day we decided to go up a mountain. So we caught the mountain train that took us about three quarters of the way up the mountain and then we walked. It didn't look that far to the top and we began walking quite quickly. It didn't take long though before we started to feel tired and there were one or two complaints from my children! One of the problems was that just as we climbed over what we thought was the last ridge, we found that we still had a long way to go.

After a while my wife and elder daughter Abbie decided they had had enough, so they sat down, and I pressed on with my younger daughter Sarah. We saw a cross on the top of the mountain, and we both wanted to reach it, but in the end Sarah was just too exhausted. I carried on. It was hard, hard work, and rather dangerous because the path was narrow and there was a steep drop either side. Eventually I made it to the cross, which was actually a viewing point. I was exhausted, but it was worth it, because I got the most amazing panoramic view of the Alps. Words cannot describe what I saw.

It was breathtaking and exhilarating, and well worth the pain of the long walk. I was so glad I had persevered.

Keep going

So keep walking with Jesus. Even when the way is hard and steep, and maybe even dangerous, keep going. What a fantastic reward is waiting for you in heaven! It is much better than breathtaking and exhilarating, and will be well worth going through the ups and downs of the Christian life.

Memory Verse

'I am the vine; you are the branches. If a man remains in me and I in him, he will bear much fruit; apart from me you can do nothing.'

John 15:5.

Time to think

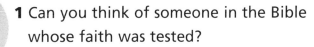

1 Can you think of someone in the Bible whose faith was tested?

2 What should we do in times of trial?

3 Think of how God might test your faith.

Time to pray

1 Ask God to give you strength to walk with him for the rest of your life.

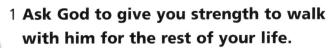

2 Pray for a Christian friend to stay close to Jesus.

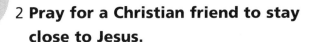

3 Ask God to save someone you know who is not a Christian.

3 Growing Up

JAMES 1:1-8

'Perseverance must finish its work so that you may be mature and complete, not lacking anything.'

'Like newborn babies, crave pure spiritual milk, so that by it you may grow up in your salvation, now that you have tasted that the Lord is good.'

1 Peter 2:2-3

So far James has told us that we are to rejoice in trials of many kinds, because the testing of our faith produces the strength of character to keep following Jesus - perseverance he called it. And perseverance leads on to maturity.

From a baby to a toddler

I expect you'll agree with me that when you were born, you were born as a baby. Nobody is born as an adult, a ridiculous thought. From the moment you were born (actually, from the moment you were conceived), you started to grow and mature. To start with, if you were hungry or thirsty, you didn't ask your mum politely, you just screamed your head off and expected mum to come running. Hopefully now you say please and

wait patiently. After what I call the screaming years, you became a toddler. You didn't jump from a baby to an adult. No! You became a toddler and went through the terrible twos when you demanded your own way and flew into a temper tantrum whenever your parents said no.

From a child to an adult

Then you became a child and went to school where you learnt to be a little more independent and sensible (hopefully!). After that, the dreaded teenage years, when you really do begin to turn into an

A piece of advice:
As you grow up, take one day at a time.

adult. At thirteen you still need mum and dad to do all sorts of things for you, although you might not like to admit it! At nineteen, you could be married and have a family of your own.

Growing up takes time

In other words, growing up takes time. You go through many different stages, and experience 'the good, bad and ugly' of life. You learn from your mistakes, from other people, from books. You become stronger and faster. Your understanding of the world becomes clearer and you start to form your own opinions. Growing up is a process, and only at the end of that process are you a responsible adult, who is ready to teach others and look after children.

Spiritual babies

The Christian life is exactly the same. We need to grow up. When we first become a Christian, we are spiritual babies, who need help with everything to do with our new life. We understand very little of the ways of God. We are easily upset and begin to doubt God. Temptation is hard to resist. The Biblc is difficult for us to understand and we need someone to explain it to us. Prayer is exciting, but we need to learn how to intercede for others and to wrestle with God. Yes, we are spiritually alive and in God's family, but we need to grow, to pass through the stages of being a spiritual toddler, child, teenager and adult, and then we can help others and lead them to the Saviour in their time of need. It's only as we pass through these stages that we become 'mature and complete, not lacking anything'.

Food and water

Naturally speaking, what helps us to grow? Well, we certainly need food and water every day. If we don't drink, we shall become terribly dehydrated, our lips will crack, and our mouths will become so dry that we will have no saliva to swallow. We shall become weak and ill and very soon die. If we don't eat, something similar will happen, it'll just take a little longer.

Spiritually speaking, we need exactly the same. We need spiritual food and water. Jesus is the bread of life and he is the water of life. We need to feed on him and drink from his spring. How do we do that? By having a daily relationship with him. By talking to him in prayer, by reading his Word, the Bible, by listening to him as he speaks to us through our parents or at church. By trusting him even when everything seems to be going wrong. By running to him and

asking for forgiveness when we sin. By thinking about his love for us and all that he has done when he died on the cross. By living lives that please him and show him that we are ready for his second coming.

Talking to Jesus

Imagine knowing a child to whom you never talk, you never listen to what they say, and you never want to be with them. You certainly couldn't call that child your friend. If Jesus is your best friend, and he must be if you are a Christian, you will talk to him, listen to what he says, and enjoy being in his presence. Otherwise, you cannot be a Christian.

If you are a Christian, why don't you set aside some time each day, perhaps before you go to school or as soon as you return home, to spend with Jesus. He is much more exciting than watching TV or playing computer games or reading a book. He is the only one who can make you grow as a Christian. So go to him every day. Pour out your heart to him. Tell him all the good things and the bad things about yourself. Tell him what worries you and what makes you happy. Be honest and real with him. Read his Word and ask him to help you understand it. Thank him and praise him for blessings and trials. And what you'll find is that without really noticing, you will grow as a Christian and become more mature and complete.

> ### Memory Verse
> 'Grow in the grace and knowledge of our Lord and Saviour Jesus Christ. To him be glory both now and for ever! Amen.'
>
> **2 Peter 3:18**

Time to think

1 Why is spending time with Jesus so important?
2 When is the best part of the day for you to spend time with Jesus?
3 What will happen if you stop reading the Bible?

Time to pray

1 **Thank God for all the good and bad times you have experienced.**
2 **Ask him to mature you through the difficulties of life.**
3 **Ask him to help you draw near to him every day.**

4 Ask God for Wisdom

JAMES 1:1-8

'If any of you lacks wisdom, he should ask God, who gives generously to all without finding fault, and it will be given to him. But when he asks, he must believe and not doubt, because he who doubts is like a wave of the sea, blown and tossed by the wind. That man should not think he will receive anything from the Lord; he is a double-minded man, unstable in all he does.'

Wisdom is not brains. Just because someone is intelligent does not mean he is wise. In fact, you can have an intelligent fool. Wisdom is using the knowledge we have to live for the glory of God. It's all to do with the kind of life we live. We shall talk more about this when we come to chapter three of James.

A wise man is able to take what he knows and use it to help others in such a way that brings praise to God. A wise man lives a life that pleases God. A wise man makes the right decisions.

Take note of this:

Solomon did not ask God for a long life, for wealth or for victory over his enemies, but for wisdom.

Solomon

Solomon was the wisest man that ever lived and for most of his life he used the wisdom that God had given him to govern his people fairly. He not only possessed great knowledge, but he used that knowledge for the good of others. He was certainly an expert decision maker.

Mrs Liar and Mrs Truth

On one occasion two women, who lived in the same house, came to King Solomon with a problem. Let's call them Mrs Liar and Mrs Truth. Both of them had had a baby boy at round about the same time. During one night Mrs Liar accidentally rolled over onto her baby and suffocated him. So she quietly got out of bed and while holding her dead baby crept into Mrs Truth's room and swapped the two babies. She tiptoed back to her room with Mrs Truth's baby. In the morning, Mrs Truth woke up and to her horror realised that her baby was dead. But when she took a closer look she saw that

it was not her baby but Mrs Liar's. Mrs Liar then shouted out in front of the king, 'No! That woman is talking nonsense. The living child is mine and the dead one is hers.'

'That's not true,' replied Mrs Truth, 'the living one is mine and the dead one is yours.' And so they argued before the king.

The king said, 'This one says, "My son is alive and your son is dead," while that one says, "No! Your son is dead and mine is alive." Bring me a sword. Cut the living baby in two and give half to Mrs Liar and half to Mrs Truth.'

Immediately Mrs Truth, who felt great love for her baby, cried out, 'Please, my lord, give her the living baby! Don't kill him!'

'Cut him in two!' yelled Mrs Liar. 'Neither of us shall have him.'

Solomon then knew whose baby it was and he gave this ruling: 'Give the living baby to Mrs Truth, for she is his mother.' And mother and son were reunited.

Solomon was using his wisdom to make important decisions and to act fairly before God.

Solomon three times over

I once read a funny story about a man who had recently joined the army and whose surname was Solomon. The sergeant came up to him one day and asked, 'Private Solomon, what's your first name?'

'Solomon,' replied Solomon.

'Oh, so you think you're a wise guy, do you?' barked the sergeant. 'What's your middle name?'

'Solomon,' replied Solomon.

The sergeant was furious and yelled at him, 'Listen here, wise guy, don't give me any of that Solomon stuff!'

But Private Solomon was only telling the truth. His full name, can you believe it, was Solomon Solomon Solomon. I wonder if he was three times as wise as King Solomon. I doubt it.

Ask God for wisdom

Now we all need more wisdom, so let us ask God for more. And when we ask, let us remember these four things: Firstly, God loves us and he loves to give good gifts to his children. Secondly, he is generous and has plenty of wisdom to give to everyone who asks for it. Thirdly, he is not going to criticise us for asking. On the contrary, he is going to be pleased, because whenever we ask God for something, we are showing him that we believe he has it and wants to give it. And fourthly, God has no favourites. Whoever we are, if we ask, trusting in him, he will give it to us.

Now it's very important that when we ask for wisdom, we must believe in God and not doubt him, otherwise we are like a wave of the sea, blown and tossed by the wind in all sorts of different directions. We are double-minded, which means that one minute we think God will give us wisdom and the next minute we think he has changed his mind and will not give it to us. We are unstable, as if

walking a tightrope and any second we are going to fall off. We should never think of God as mean or unwilling to help us. That is to insult him.

When you pray, remember that Jesus possesses all the treasures of wisdom and knowledge and can give them to anyone he chooses. He is kind and generous and has never yet refused anyone who came to him sincerely and in faith.

Time to think

1 What is wisdom?

2 Why do we need it?

3 Can you think of a wise decision that Jesus made?

Time to pray

1 **Ask God to give you a strong faith.**

2 **Ask him to give you wisdom so you can live your life for his glory.**

3 **Pray for someone you know who has a difficult decision to make.**

5 Are you Rich or Poor?

JAMES 1:9-11

'The brother in humble circumstances ought to take pride in his high position. But the one who is rich should take pride in his low position, because he will pass away like a wild flower. For the sun rises with scorching heat and withers the plant; its blossom falls and its beauty is destroyed. In the same way, the rich man will fade away even while he goes about his business.'

Are you rich or poor? I suppose it depends who you compare yourself with. If you think of a millionaire, then you are not rich. But if you think of many millions throughout the world who live well below the poverty line, then you are rich.

Very poor

Let's just pretend for a moment that you are very poor. In other words, as James says, you live in 'humble circumstances'. Your mud hut home is about the size of a garden shed, you have no running water or electricity, and the school you go to is a five-mile walk away. You have no bicycle, you've never heard of television, and as for a computer, you think that is something an alien might use! The food you eat every day is boiled rice, and if a member of your family becomes ill, there is no doctor within twenty miles. You

> Think for a minute about the poverty of Jesus.

sleep on the dirt floor and have to go to the river to wash.

Very poor but very rich

Now the wonderful news of the gospel is that even if you are that poor, if you are a Christian, you are rich beyond compare. Oh, I don't mean you have lots of money and possessions. I mean you are spiritually rich. For one thing, you are in God's family. What an amazing privilege to belong to that family! You can call God Father and you are his child. Just as you know your own parents, so you know the living God, the Creator of the heavens and the earth, the God that so many people are trying to find through their own efforts or religions.

You can talk to God

Not only that, but you can talk to him. Imagine if you wanted to speak to the Queen of England or the President of the USA. Would it be possible? You couldn't just pick up the telephone and have a chat with them. Do you know their

number? I doubt it. But even if you did, you would never get through to them. Their secretary would answer and almost certainly refuse to put you through to them, as you are a 'nobody', if you don't mind me using that word. But you can speak to God and it's easier than picking up a telephone and dialling the number. You can tell God anything you want to and he will be interested because he loves you. He is never busy or out so you can't reach him. Is the president really interested in you? Does he love you? Can he answer all your requests? Does the queen even know your name? How rich you are to be able to talk to the Almighty Saviour.

Your sins are forgiven

Your sins are also forgiven, thrown as far as the east is from the west. Now your life is whiter than snow. Speaking of snow, just the other day we had a heavy snow shower and as we get so little snow in Bournemouth, my family and I quickly ran out into it and had a snowball fight. We also built a snowman, which was only about 50cm high, but it had a body, a head and two eyes and a mouth. There was not enough snow to make a bigger one. For a couple of days it stood proudly in our garden until the thaw began, and before we knew it, it had disappeared. We knew where it had been standing, but it had gone. We could have searched for it all day and night and in every corner of the garden, but we would not have found it. It had gone for ever.

That is just what happens to our sins when we become a Christian. They melt away like a snowman before the rising sun. The blood of Jesus washes them away for good and we shall never find them again. Even if we search and search for them, we will never find them. Now if forgiveness does not make us rich, then I don't know what does. All who have not been forgiven are going to have to suffer eternally under the wrath of God. But thanks to Jesus and his death on the cross, every believer has been forgiven and our future is secure in heaven.

Are you a Christian?
Before I go on, ask yourself this question: Am I a Christian? Have I been forgiven? If your answer is no, turn to Jesus now. Before you read on, bow your head and ask God to forgive you for all the things you've done wrong. Thank him for Jesus, the Saviour of the world, who has made it possible for God to forgive you. He will not turn you away or refuse to wash your sins away.

Can you see how incredibly rich even a very poor Christian is? He has everything he needs to enjoy life and glorify God.

Memory Verse

'For you know the grace of our Lord Jesus Christ, that though he was rich, yet for your sakes he became poor, so that you through his poverty might become rich.'

2 Corinthians 8:9

Are you a rich Christian?
But if you are a rich Christian, with three houses and five cars, and large amounts of money stashed away in banks and building societies, remember this: your life will not last for ever. One day you will die and you will not be able to take one penny with you to heaven. Just as the plant is withered by the sun and its blossoms fall and its beauty is destroyed, so you will fade away as you go about your business. You may be very young at the moment, and have everything you can possibly want, but your life will one day end, and you should never forget that. It may be sooner than you think. Such thoughts should humble you and make you fully dependent on God, who holds your life and death in his hands. Never behave as if you are indestructible, but trust in God and look to him for your every breath. He gives life and he takes it away whenever he chooses. Therefore, 'take pride in your low position', that you are as weak and helpless as everyone else, and turn to the Lord with renewed devotion.

Time to think
1 Why is it so hard for a rich person to enter the kingdom of heaven?
2 What spiritual advantages do poor people have over the rich?
3 Apart from what I've mentioned, what other ways are poor Christians rich towards God?

Time to pray
1 **Thank God for all the material possessions he has given you.**
2 **Ask him to help you depend only on him.**
3 **Pray for someone you know or have heard about who is very poor.**

6 A Bruising Journey

JAMES 1:12-18

'Blessed is the man who perseveres under trial, because when he has stood the test, he will receive the crown of life that God has promised to those who love him.'

The Chinese have a proverb, which says:

'A journey of a thousand miles begins with one step.'

The Christian's journey to heaven can be a bruising affair. Sometimes the tunnels we have to walk through on our way to heaven are long and dark and there seems to be no light at the end of them. Our path is full of snares and pot holes and temptations and we often trip over the many obstacles in our way. There are times of disappointment and sadness, even heartbreak. A lovely Christian family I know came home one day to find their teenage son hanging by his neck in the garden. All attempts to resuscitate him failed and their lives have never been the same since.

366
Pain and illness are always difficult to bear, especially if they are prolonged and there is no medical cure. Fear is a constant thorn in the flesh for many. I have not counted them, but I have been told that there are 366 'fear nots' in the Bible. One for each day of the year. God tells us every day not to fear, but to trust in him. Perhaps you are being bullied at school, or you have an unhappy home life, or there are other relationships in your life that are going wrong and making you feel unhappy. These things hurt us and make our journey to heaven difficult.

Moses
Consider the great men of God in the Bible and all the troubles they encountered. Take Moses for an example. As a baby he only just escaped being thrown into the River Nile. When he was forty he had to flee from the king of Egypt, who wanted to kill him. Forty years later he returned to Egypt and was used by God to set his people free. No easy task! He then had to put up with a grumbling, disobedient and insolent people for the rest of his life!

Joseph and David
Or what about Joseph and David? Joseph was thrown into a cistern by his brothers, sold as a slave,

Now this is good advice:
'Encourage one another daily, as long as it is called Today, so that none of you may be hardened by sin's deceitfulness.'

Hebrew 3:13

falsely accused and put in prison. David, as a boy, had to overcome the giant Goliath. Then he was hunted like an animal by the jealous and angry King Saul, and later even his own son turned against him.

What do these three men have in common? They kept following God and did not give up. They weren't perfect and they made many mistakes and committed many sins, but they persevered and in the end they received their reward, the crown of life.

Let me pass on four pieces of advice: Firstly, when you are discouraged and feel like giving up because the Christian life is too hard, think about the three men I have mentioned and how they remained faithful in spite of all their difficulties. I expect their problems were much worse than the problems you and I experience.

You are weak, God is strong

Secondly, remember that we live the Christian life not in our own strength, but with the strength God gives us. He is our strength and power. So when you feel weak, run to him and he will lift you up. He is faithful to his children. In Isaiah 40:29-31 it says these comforting words:

'He gives strength to the weary and increases the power of the weak. Even youths grow tired and weary, and young men stumble and fall; but those who hope in the Lord will renew their strength. They will soar on wings like eagles; they will run and not grow weary, they will walk and not be faint.'

Jesus

Thirdly, consider Jesus. He is not only our Lord and Saviour, but he is our perfect example. When life is really tough, think about Jesus on the cross, an innocent man being punished for the sins of the world. Think about how they beat him and spat in his face, and whipped him and thrust a crown of thorns onto his head. Think about him carrying his own cross to the place of execution, the nails being hammered into his hands and feet, the bystanders laughing at him, the soldiers gambling for his clothes. Think about how his Father turned his back on him, how he was crushed for our sins. Listen to the words he cried out from the cross when in utmost agony of body and soul. Feel the earthquake shake the ground. Watch as the three hours of darkness covered him and the soldier pierced his side with a spear. See him bow his head in

death, the pure and spotless Lamb of God who takes away the sins of the world. And then tell yourself, 'What I am suffering is nothing compared to the sufferings of Jesus. He endured the most terrible death so that I could be saved from hell, the devil, the wrath of God, my sins. I shall follow him all the days of my life, come what may.'

The prize

And finally, think about the prize you will receive at the end of your journey, the crown of life. I recently watched England beat Australia in the Rugby World Cup Final. It was tough for England. Australia kept coming back at them. England were tired, battered and bruised, but they kept fighting with all their might. They did not give up. Why? Because they wanted to win the World Cup and receive the trophy. And when they finally won, all the training and pain were worth it. They were the champions of the world.

As Christians, we do not fight for a trophy that will one day be taken from us. No, we fight for 'the crown of life that God has promised to those who love him'. It's an eternal crown, a priceless crown, a glorious crown and no one can snatch it from us. That's why we are blessed if we persevere under trial. So follow Jesus wholeheartedly through thick and thin. Never be discouraged in your Christian journey, just hold on to your Master Jesus and he will see you to the end.

> ### Memory Verse
> 'Let us not become weary in doing good, for at the proper time we will reap a harvest if we do not give up.'
>
> **Galatians 6:9**

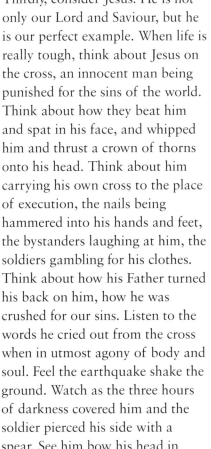

Time to think

1 Who in the New Testament suffered greatly for their Christian faith?

2 How many of the seven words that Jesus spoke from the cross can you name?

3 What does it mean to persevere?

Time to pray

1 **Rededicate yourself to God.**

2 **Ask him to help you stop complaining about difficulties and to start praising him for his grace and mercy.**

3 **Ask him to make the cross and all that it means more real to you.**

7

Say, 'No!'

JAMES 1:12-18

'When tempted, no one should say, "God is tempting me." For God cannot be tempted by evil, nor does he tempt anyone; but each one is tempted when, by his own evil desire, he is dragged away and enticed. Then, after desire has conceived, it gives birth to sin; and sin, when it is full-grown, gives birth to death.'

When we are tempted to do wrong we can be absolutely sure that it is not God who is tempting us, for 'God cannot be tempted by evil, nor does he tempt anyone'. Rather, we are being tempted by our own evil desires. In each one of us there is that desire to do wrong and to do the opposite of what God has commanded. If God tells us not to do something, we find in us a pulling towards the very thing that God has forbidden.

Don't touch!

It's a bit like if we're going for a walk and we read a sign that says KEEP OUT! What is our reaction? We want to go in and see why we should keep out. Have you ever walked past a sign that read 'Wet paint. Don't touch'? And did you reach out your little finger to see if the paint was really wet? A couple of weeks ago I went out for a Chinese meal with my wife. The waitress brought the plates and said, 'Be careful, the plates are very hot.' What do you think I did next? Yes, you're right. I put my hands on the plate in front of me to see just how hot it was.

> **If you're going to fight a battle, you need protection:**
>
> 'Finally be strong in the Lord and in his mighty power. Put on the full armour of God so that you can take your stand against the devil's schemes.'
>
> **Ephesians 6:10-11**

Thankfully I did not burn myself, but if I had burnt myself, I would only have one person to blame.

Say, 'No!'

Each one of us has a sinful nature that desires all those things that God has forbidden. Therefore we need to arm ourselves to fight against temptation and to say NO! to it when it appears. To live a godly life is a battle. If you were going out to fight your enemy, who was determined to kill you, you would arm yourself and wear protective clothing. You would put

a helmet on and wear a bullet proof jacket. You would take a loaded gun with you and keep your eyes wide open so you could spot him if he crept up on you. As soon as you saw him, you would run and hide or try to kill him first.

Run as fast as you can

It's the same with temptation. We must fight against it with all our might and put on the whole armour of God. As soon as we see it lurking in the bushes ready to pounce, we must run to Jesus our shield and hide behind him. If necessary, we should act like Joseph, who literally ran out of the house, leaving his cloak behind when he was being tempted by Potiphar's wife. I remember reading about a slave who had to pass a field full of watermelons on his way to and from work. Every day he was tempted to go into the field and steal a watermelon. So every time he reached the field he ran as fast as he could until the field was out of sight. He told his friends, 'I can't stop my mouth from watering at the sight of those melons, but I can run fast.'

Bob's bathing costume

We should not make any provision for giving in to temptation. Never behave like Bob. Bob's mother told him that under no circumstances was he allowed to swim in a nearby pond. She thought it was dangerous and Bob was not a very good swimmer. The next time Bob passed by the pond he took his bathing costume with him. His friend asked him, 'Why have you brought your bathing costume with you?'

'Just in case I get tempted,' replied Bob. Now that is NOT the way to resist temptation. If anything Bob should have destroyed his bathing costume, or taken a different path that went nowhere near the pond, or he should have acted like that slave and run past the pond. Instead, by taking his costume, he was preparing to say YES to the temptation.

Watch and pray

I think one of the best ways to say NO to temptation is to prepare yourself by watching and praying. Temptations come upon us suddenly and if we are not watching they can catch us out. When I went to Africa to watch the wild animals in their natural habitat, one thing I noticed was that animals like gazelles, whenever they drank at a water hole, would take a quick sip and then look up and all around. When they thought it was safe, they would take another quick sip and then immediately look up and around again. They knew only too well that their enemies were waiting for an unguarded moment to pounce on them. We should be like that with temptation. Watch out, there's a temptation about.

The ice cream van

But we should pray as well and ask God to help us say NO and to 'lead us not into temptation'. A young boy Alexander was saving all his money in order to buy a new football, but he was finding it very hard not to spend his money on sweets and ice cream. One night, as he was praying, his mother heard him say, with a hint of desperation, 'O Lord, please help me save my money to buy a new football. And please, Lord, don't let the ice cream van come down my street!'

When we pray we are focusing on the holy God and drawing on his strength. We are, quite simply, asking for his help, and he always responds to that sort of prayer. So watch carefully and pray hard because our evil desires will pull us away from God and draw us into sin, 'and sin, when it is full-grown, gives birth to death'.

Time to think

1 What is the difference between temptation and sin?

2 How did Jesus resist temptation?

3 What should we do to live holy lives?

Time to pray

1 **Repent of the times you have given in to temptation.**

2 **Ask God to help you resist temptation.**

3 **Ask him to make you inwardly and outwardly holy.**

8 God is Good

> 'Don't be deceived, my dear brothers. Every good and perfect gift is from above, coming down from the Father of the heavenly lights, who does not change like shifting shadows.'

One thing we can be absolutely sure about is that God is good. Even if everyone and everything around us is bad all the time, we can look up to God and see that he is different in every way, that he is good all of the time - his character is good, his thoughts are good, his plans are good, his Word is good; everything about him is good.

God is good in all he does and says

Now because God's nature is good, what he does and says is good. Take creation as an example. After God had created all that he wanted to create he examined it and saw that it was 'very good'. One of the best things about creation for me is that God created Adam and Eve on day six and not on day one. In other words, he got everything ready first - the land and seas, vegetation and light, fish and birds and animals - so that when he made Adam and Eve they could live a happy and secure life.

Now I know this is a bit silly, but imagine they had been created first. They would have had to swim around in the darkness, with nothing to eat until God had made everything else. Yes, it would have

These are Jesus' actual words:

'I am the good shepherd; I know my sheep and my sheep know me — just as the Father knows me and I know the Father — and I lay down my life for the sheep.'

John 10:14-15

been for six days only, but even so, just imagine swimming non-stop until day three when land was formed. Then they would have had to dry themselves off and start searching for food. As it was everything was made ready for them. It was as if God had laid the table, cooked all the food and was ready to serve them. All they had to do was sit down and eat.

The Good Shepherd

The reason God does good things is because he is good. There is no better example of God's goodness than when he sent his Son into the world to save sinners. It was not as if we deserved it, or that God had no other choice. He could have left us in our sins to suffer his wrath eternally. But he sent Jesus to rescue us, to open our blinded eyes to his goodness, to unstop our deaf ears to the words of eternal life, to soften our hard hearts to his love and to turn us back to himself. The reason why you are reading this book is because God is good and he wants to teach you more about himself. Remember, Jesus called himself the good shepherd, because he cares for the sheep, and lays down his life for them. When you read through the four gospels you cannot fail to see that Jesus went around doing good to others, healing the broken-hearted, setting captives free, curing diseases, feeding the hungry, forgiving the repentant and so on.

God never changes

Now you might ask, 'Is there any chance of God becoming bad?' The answer to that is no because God 'does not change like shifting shadows'. If you stand in the sun, your shadow will change. It will get bigger or smaller or move around and point in another direction. If the sun is behind a cloud, you won't have any shadow! But God is not like your shadow. He never changes. He is eternally good. That means we can always trust him, we can always run to him for help.

Now because God is always good, we know that when he sends difficulties and sorrows into our lives, it is for our good, that we will rely on him more completely. When we face 'trials of many kinds', we must never think it is because God has become bad or that he is afflicting us for bad reasons. No! Again, think of Jesus. God caused him to suffer so that he could save countless millions of people from hell. That is why it says in Hebrews that Jesus endured the cross for the 'joy set before him', the joy of seeing so many rescued from Satan's kingdom, men and women, boys and girls, whose transformed lives bring glory to God.

Two hungry children

One other thing that I must mention is that God enables you and me to do good to others. I remember hearing a missionary to India relate the following story. He was walking down one of the dirty back streets of a very poor area when two children, a brother and sister, came up to him, looking very hungry. At the time he only had half a loaf of bread on him so he willingly gave it to them. They both smiled at him and ran off down the street and sat down under a small bridge. The missionary stood and watched them for a while. He saw the boy, who must have been about eight years old, give the bread to his younger sister, and as she ate he just watched. Although he was very hungry, he did not eat one crumb until his sister had eaten as much as she wanted, and then he ate the small piece that was left over. You see, he loved his sister and wanted her to satisfy her hunger first. It was an act of kindness and goodness.

You and I can do good things to others. We don't always have to be selfish and greedy. We can share and be kind. But it is only God who enables us to think of others before ourselves, because all the good in the world comes from him. Without him, we would never do good to anyone.

Time to think

1 Why can't God ever be bad?

2 Name examples of God's goodness in the Bible.

3 How has God been good to you?

Time to pray

1 **Praise God that he is eternally good.**

2 **Thank him for sending his Son into the world.**

3 **Ask him to help you be good to others.**

Listen

JAMES 1:19-27

'My dear brothers, take note of this: Everyone should be quick to listen, slow to speak and slow to become angry, for man's anger does not bring about the righteous life that God desires.'

Whether you are at school or home or somewhere else it is vital that you are 'quick to listen' to what you are told. 'Why?' you ask. Because you might hear something that could save your life.

A fighter pilot

Imagine you are a fighter pilot in one of those really fast jets. I expect you know that those aeroplanes have an ejector seat, so that if the plane is in trouble and about to crash the pilot can catapult himself out of the cockpit. His parachute will then open automatically and he will float safely to the ground. Now imagine you have been through your training, and for most of the time you have been listening carefully. But when your instructor was talking about the ejector seat and which button to press in the cockpit, you were whispering something to your neighbour and having a bit of a laugh with him. Besides, you thought that you

would never get into trouble because you were such a good pilot.

One day, as you are flying around at very fast speeds, going through various exercises, there is a bang and a crunch from one of the plane's engines. You notice smoke pouring from it and you begin to panic. You look across to the other engine and that seems OK, but all the while you are losing height. You try desperately to gain height but the controls do not respond. You think you will have to eject. But then you have an awful thought. 'Where is the ejector button?' You think back to your lessons and you rack your brains to try and recall what your instructor said. Suddenly you remember that when you were being taught about the safety measures, you were busy talking to your neighbour. Now you really start to panic. You look all around the cockpit, under your seat, behind you and you can't find the button anywhere. The cockpit

Do not be like the men in the Sanhedrin, who were listening to Stephen preach. What did they do? They covered their ears and yelled at the top of their voices so they could not hear what he said.

Acts 7:57

is beginning to fill with smoke and it's getting hard to see. You cry out to yourself, 'If only I had listened! Help!' And that's the last that is heard from you.

Listen to the words of Jesus

I hope that story illustrates just how important it is to listen. Now, how much more important it is to listen to the words of Jesus, who tells you the way to eternal life. What terrible consequences there are if you do not listen to him! Do you realise that if you do not listen to the words of Jesus, you will not know how to escape from hell? If you are not a Christian, you are walking on the road that leads to hell, you are lost. What a fool you are, if your friend or parents tell you about Jesus and that he is the way to escape eternal punishment, but you don't listen to what they say! If you read the Bible, but don't really pay attention to its message, what good is it to you? Only Jesus Christ can save you and you need to listen to his instructions.

The market bell

We must be very careful that we are not like the crowd who was listening to a musician play on the street. That musician thought he was holding his audience spell bound by the beautiful sounds that were coming from his violin, but there was a market being set up nearby. As soon as the market bell sounded to indicate it was open, all but one of his listeners rushed off to the market to try and buy some special deals. The violinist went up to his one remaining admirer, and said, 'Thank you for not rushing away at the sound of the market bell and for prizing beautiful music above material possessions.'

The old man replied, 'I'm sorry, but I'm hard of hearing. Did you say the market bell has gone?'

'Yes,' said the musician.

'Then I must be off,' said the old man, and he quickly hurried off down the road.

Are you deaf?

Sometimes we can be so taken up with what the world offers, that we won't or cannot hear the words of Jesus. We perhaps listen for a short time, but when something more attractive appears, we are off to satisfy our lusts. Take note of this: Nothing is more important than the words of Jesus.

Be 'slow to speak'

James also says that we should be 'slow to speak'. Isn't it hard to speak and listen at the same time? Have you ever had a conversation with someone and you both start speaking at the same time and neither of you want to stop because you are more interested in speaking than in listening? The conversation ends up in a right mess and neither of you make sense of nor hear what the other is saying. At all times we need to listen carefully to what others say and to think before we speak.

Be 'slow to become angry'

We must also be 'slow to become angry', because the last thing we do when we are in a rage is listen.

What happened the last time you lost your temper? You probably shouted and screamed and refused to listen to what anyone else was saying. I heard of a boy, who got into such a rage that he shouted his head off, threw all the chairs around his classroom, and then started to strangle another boy. Was he in any shape to listen carefully to what others were saying? No!

Our anger does not 'bring about the righteous life that God desires'. When we are angry we say and do the most horrible things. We hurt others and we hurt ourselves. We do not 'love our neighbour as ourselves', but do the exact opposite. These things should not be.

Time to think

1 Why should we be quick to listen?

2 Why should we be slow to speak?

3 When we're angry, what sort of things do we do that displease God?

Time to pray

1 Repent of the times when you have not listened to the Word of God.

2 Ask God to show you the importance of his Word.

3 Pray that God will speak to you as you read the Bible.

10 Throw it Away

JAMES 1:19-27

'Get rid of all moral filth and the evil that is so prevalent, and humbly accept the word planted in you, which can save you.'

What do you do after you have been playing football or netball or some other sport and you go into the changing room covered in mud? I'm sure you don't just jump into your mum and dad's clean car, with your dirty clothes and muddy boots, and drive home. If you do, I'm sure you don't sit down on your parents' expensive sofa, put your feet up, and with wet mud still dripping from your boots, watch a bit of telly. If you do, I'm sure you don't sit down at the table and eat your sandwiches with filthy hands and then climb into bed with your games kit and boots still on. Of course not!

As soon as the game is over, you take off your dirty clothes, give them to someone to clean and

jump into the shower. When you come out of the shower, you don't put your dirty clothes back on or your dirty boots. No, you put on clean clothes and a clean pair of shoes. I expect your friends would think you were mad if you put on your dirty clothes after your shower.

Disgusting!

When I was about ten years old my family and I lived in a cul-de-sac, with some twenty other families. I soon got friendly with another boy my age and we used to play a lot together. Sometimes we got into trouble. Would you believe me if I said that my friend was always leading me astray? No? Well, you would be quite right! It was six of one and half a dozen of the other. Down one end of the cul-de-sac was a sewage works, where they used to treat human waste and turn it into manure. It was strictly forbidden to go into the works and there were signs everywhere telling us to keep out. Our parents had also told us not to play anywhere near the place.

But for two ten year old boys it seemed a very exciting place to play, especially as there was an element of risk involved, with the

What does the Bible say?

'But now you must rid yourselves of all such things as these: anger, rage, malice, slander and filthy language from your lips.'

Colossians 3:8

Sin is disgusting in the sight of God; therefore, throw it away.

possibility of being found out. So one day we decided to have a look round. We squeezed through the fence and started to explore. It was good fun. Any time we saw someone, we ducked behind a wall and made sure we were not seen. It was a bit like playing soldiers and we were avoiding the enemy. But then something awful happened.

Around the site were large containers that had been dug into the ground. The top of them was at ground level so they were easy to look into. One particular container that we peered into looked empty. We were sure it had a solid bottom, so we decided to jump in and investigate. My friend went first. To his horror, the container did not have a solid bottom, but was half full of the most disgusting and foul smelling human waste. He went right under and then started to panic because he did not know how to swim. He shouted out to me, but there was no way I was going to jump into all that excrement to save him, so I shouted back, 'Swim!' And swim he did. In fact, he learnt to swim in all that human waste.

He managed to reach the side and I leant down to pull him out. He was absolutely filthy, from head to foot, and he stunk. He staggered home, crying bitterly, and hardly expecting to survive the anger of his parents. As soon as he got home he ripped off his clothes, threw them in the bin and washed like he had never washed before.

Disobedience stinks
Now when James says 'get rid of all moral filth and the evil that is so prevalent', he is telling us to rip off our foul smelling clothes of selfishness, rudeness, lust, temper tantrums, lies etc, and to throw them away for ever. Instead we are to ask God for forgiveness and to put on behaviour that is in line with God's Word. Do you realise that disobedience stinks? It is a repulsive smell to God. It is the stench of death. Whereas obedience is a sweet fragrance to God, an aroma that he enjoys and can bless.

Obey God's Word
In other words, don't just listen to the Word of God, obey it. Put it into practice. If it tells us to be 'slow to become angry', then ask God to give you the grace and humility not to be quick tempered or to react aggressively to provocation. When it tells us to ask God for wisdom, ask him, knowing that he gives generously to all without finding fault. If you put God's Word into practice, you are like the wise man who built his house on the rock. You will be able to stand firm when the day of trouble comes.

Throw away your filthy rags
One final thought. When you put on some new clothes, you first have to take off the old ones. You never put new clothes over the old ones. That would be too uncomfortable and the new clothes would not fit properly. Before we can put on the armour of God, with which we fight against the devil and his schemes, we must throw away the filthy rags of our old life. Only then can we fight effectively against the enemy of our souls.

Time to think

1 Name those areas of your life where you are obeying the Word of God.

2 Name those areas of your life where you are not obeying the Word of God.

3 Why do we find it hard to obey?

Time to pray

1 **Ask God to forgive you for your disobedience.**

2 **Ask him to help you stand up for what is right at school.**

3 **Pray for someone in your class to become a Christian.**

11 Listen and Obey

JAMES 1:19-27

'Do not merely listen to the word, and so deceive yourselves. Do what it says. Anyone who listens to the word but does not do what it says is like a man who looks at his face in a mirror and, after looking at himself, goes away and immediately forgets what he looks like. But the man who looks intently into the perfect law that gives freedom, and continues to do this, not forgetting what he has heard, but doing it — he will be blessed in what he does.'

?? Question ??

Is there any point in reading God's Word, if you do not obey it?

If we simply listen to the Word of God, but do not put it into practice, we are really saying several things. We are saying that the Word of God is not very important, and that is why it does not need to be obeyed. In fact, we are going further than that, we are saying that we do not believe it is the Word of God. If we honestly believe that the Bible is the Word of God, we would do all in our power to obey it, for it is the Word of the Creator and the Ruler of heaven and earth. We try to obey the laws of the land, which have been passed by our government, because they are important and we realise they are for our protection. How much more should we obey the Word of the Almighty and sovereign God in whose hands all things lie.

It is dangerous not to obey

I will go further. If we do not obey the Word of God, we are saying that our word is better. What a terrible thing to say! The word of a rebellious and wicked sinner is better than the Word of the Holy One! The word of an ignorant and spiritually blind wretch is better than the Word of the all-seeing, all-knowing God. Actually, if we only listen to the Word of God and do not obey it, we are calling God a liar. Why? Because we do not believe what God has said. And if we do not believe what God has said, he must be wrong. Are you beginning to see how dangerous it is not to put into practice the living and eternal Word of God?

30mph or 90mph?

Not only that, but just as the laws of the land are for our protection and blessing, so the laws of God are for our protection and blessing, if we obey them. Why is there a 30mph speed limit through town centres? Let me ask another question. Why can't your mum and dad drive at 90mph through a busy shopping area? The answer is obvious. Because they are likely to injure or kill innocent shoppers and themselves. Why does God's Word say we should not murder? Why can't we murder our enemies? Because if we do, we shall not only hurt the person we murder, but his family and friends as well, and we shall be put into prison for life, or in some countries executed. So God's laws are there for our protection and blessing, and in obeying them there is life and happiness.

He suddenly went blind

I once read about a young pilot who had only just got his pilot's licence. One day he went flying and was enjoying himself fairly near the airfield, when he suddenly went blind. As you can imagine, for a few minutes he panicked and did not know what to do. He thought he was going to die. After a short while he managed to gain his composure and radioed to the control tower and told them what had happened. The air traffic controller told him to listen very carefully to his instructions and to do *everything* he told him — nothing was to be disobeyed. From looking closely at his radar screen and out of the control tower window, the controller was able to see the blind pilot.

The air traffic controller gave the pilot precise instructions as to what to do. He told him when to lose height, when to bank, when to lower his flaps, when to reduce speed and so on. Whatever instructions he gave, the pilot obeyed to the letter. Amazingly, that pilot was able to land safely and his life was saved — all because he obeyed the word of the controller. How foolish it would have been for the pilot to say, 'Listen, Mr Air Traffic Controller, I can fly this plane perfectly well and I don't need your help. I am not going to obey your instructions, but do what I think best.' Not only would he have killed himself, but he may well have killed others also.

When we obey God, we are protecting others and ourselves. Obedience brings blessing, whereas disobedience is disastrous.

Do you ever look at yourself in a mirror?

James says that anyone who listens to the Word of God, but does not put it into practice is like a man who looks at himself in the mirror and then immediately forgets what he looks like. Imagine looking at yourself in the mirror and you see there is a dirty black splodge all over your left cheek. What do you do? Do you turn away and then forget it's there? No. You spend a few minutes washing it off because you do not want to go to school looking like that. When you look into the Word of God and find that it tells you that something you are doing is wrong, if you ignore it and carry on living as you please, you are a fool. But if you, with God's grace and strength, determine never to do it again, you will be 'blessed'.

I'm sure as you grow up you want to live under the blessing of God. Then obey his Word. There is no surer way to live a happy life than to do what the Master says.

The prophet Samuel said this:

'Does the LORD delight in burnt offerings and sacrifices as much as in obeying the voice of the LORD? To obey is better than sacrifice, and to heed is better than the fat of rams.'

1 Samuel 15:22

Time to think

1 Why is it important to obey God?

2 Who in the Bible was blessed for obeying God?

3 What are you saying about God's Word if you disobey it?

Time to pray

1 **Thank God for giving you the Bible.**

2 **Ask him to give you a love and a respect for the Bible.**

3 **Ask him to make you like Jesus, who always obeyed his Father.**

JAMES 1:19-27

> 'If anyone considers himself religious and yet does not keep a tight rein on his tongue, he deceives himself and his religion is worthless.'

The trouble with our tongues is they waggle too much and too easily. That's why we need to hold on to them. I sometimes think we should literally hold our tongues with our fingers so they don't move and speak so freely. Give them half a chance and they speak. Give them an inch and they take a mile. If we command them to stop speaking, they still whisper under our breaths or murmur silently. Perhaps we should nail our tongues to our jaws to keep them under control. A painful solution! They are in every sense as slippery as an eel and like the crafty serpent in the Garden of Eden.

Did you know?

'But I tell you that men will have to give account on the day of judgment for every careless word they have spoken. For by your words you will be acquitted, and by your words you will be condemned.'

Matthew 12:36-37

Have you ever been horse riding?

If you've ever been horse riding you will know that you sit on a saddle and hold onto the reins. The reins are attached to a metal bit in the horse's mouth and so by pulling on the reins you can direct the horse and keep it under control. If you pull back on the reins the horse will stop, if it's well trained! If you pull on the left rein, the horse should turn left. I'm certainly not an expert rider, but I think it is important to hold the reins tightly so that you are in command of the horse at all times and there is less risk of it suddenly running wild.

We must keep a tight rein on our tongues — that is, we must not give them too much freedom or allow them to get out of control. Like a runaway horse, once we lose control of them, they are very hard to catch and can do a great deal of damage.

Jesus always said the right thing

Jesus always kept his tongue under perfect control. He always said the right thing at the right time. He did not speak even one wrong word. Everything he said was true and right. Even when he became

Listen to this:

'Reckless words pierce like a sword, but the tongue of the wise brings healing.'

Proverbs 12:18

angry in the temple or at the Pharisees, he was still in perfect control of his tongue and never said anything that was unfair or untrue. Wouldn't it be wonderful to be like Jesus?

Words hurt

There's a well-known saying and it goes like this: Sticks and stones may break my bones, but words can never hurt me. What a lot of rubbish that is! I expect you have been hurt, perhaps deeply, by the words of someone else, and I expect you have hurt others with the words you have used. Sticks and stones may break your bones, but the wounds they cause generally heal much more quickly than the wounds caused by a hurtful tongue. Words can wound very deeply and the scars they cause can be carried for years.

The tongue is like a knife

In many ways the tongue is like a two-edged sword or knife. One side of it can be used by your enemy to stab you so that you bleed to death, while the other side of it can be used by your doctor to cut out an abscess or a cancer and so restore you to life. With our tongues we can say the most horrible and hate-filled words, and with those same tongues we can say beautiful words of blessing.

The letter 'H'

The tongue reminds me of the letter 'H'. On the one hand, it can hate, hurt and be an instrument of hell. On the other hand, it can heal, help, and bring happiness, and sound like the wonders of heaven. One minute it sings like the choirs in heaven, the next it spews out filth like the demons in hell. It's not very big, but it sure has a lot to say for itself, and so much of what it says is contradictory.

Two fools?

In the Talmud, the body of Jewish law, there is a legend about a king who called upon two men who he thought were fools. In instructing them, he said, 'Foolish Simon, I want you to search throughout my kingdom and bring me the best thing in the world.' He then spoke to Silly John, 'Go and search throughout my kingdom and find me the worst thing in the world.' So both men went and began their search.

It didn't take either man very long to find what he was looking for. Simon approached the king first and bowed before him with a grin on his face and presented his package. 'Sir,' he said, 'I have searched throughout your kingdom and I have found the best thing in the world.' The king was rather surprised that he had finished his search so soon, but he took the package. When he opened it, he found it contained a tongue.

John then approached the king and said, 'Sir, I have searched throughout your kingdom and I have found the worst thing in the world.' He too presented his package to the king. The king was even more surprised. He quickly opened the package and to his amazement there was another tongue.

Now the king might have thought that both Simon and John were fools, but in fact they had a correct knowledge of what is the best and worst thing in the world. How many times, I wonder, have you been upset by what someone has said to you? Words can make us cry and they can make us angry. And how many times have you laughed at the words of another and felt blessed? Words can make us happy.

Hold onto your tongue

So now you know the power of the tongue, set a guard over it. Keep a tight rein on it. Do not allow it to move too often. And if you are tempted to strike with your tongue, clap your hand over your mouth and do not speak. Once the words are out, they can never be taken back in.

> **Memory Verse**
> 'When words are many, sin is not absent, but he who holds his tongue is wise.'
> **Proverbs 10:19**

Time to think

1 Can you remember saying something hurtful to a member of your family?
2 Can you remember some kind words you have said?
3 Think of something Jesus said that made someone happy

Time to pray

1 **Repent of the many hurtful things you have said.**
2 **Ask God to help you keep a tight rein on your tongue.**
3 **Pray for someone you have hurt.**

13 'Don't Show Favouritism'

JAMES 2:1-4

'My brothers, as believers in our glorious Lord Jesus Christ, don't show favouritism. Suppose a man comes into your meeting wearing a gold ring and fine clothes, and a poor man in shabby clothes also comes in. If you show special attention to the man wearing fine clothes and say, "Here's a good seat for you," but say to the poor man, "You stand there" or "Sit on the floor by my seat," have you not discriminated among yourselves and become judges with evil thoughts?'

Mr Tidy

Suppose two men came to your house and stood before you. The first man we'll call Mr Tidy because he looked very clean and tidy. He had shaved and washed that morning, and brushed his hair and teeth. He wore a new suit and tie and his shoes were nice and shiny. He wore what looked like quite an expensive watch and a couple of rings on his fingers. He had obviously put on deodorant because he smelt fresh. Everything about him went along with his name Mr Tidy.

Mr Scruffy

The second man we'll call Mr Scruffy, because he looked scruffy. He had not shaved or washed that morning. His hair was sticking up at strange angles, which suggested he had been sleeping outside. He wore a crumpled T-shirt, which had two small tears in it and it certainly needed a wash. His shoes hadn't been cleaned for what

looked like years and one of them had a small hole at the end where his toe poked through. He didn't wear a watch or any rings and he looked rather poor. He was rightly called Mr Scruffy.

Now my question to you is this: If these two men stood before you, which one could you trust more, Mr Tidy or Mr Scruffy? If you said Mr Tidy, then say why you chose him. If you chose Mr Scruffy, then say why you chose him. When I asked this question at school

during a morning assembly, most children put up their hands to say they could trust Mr Tidy more. When I asked why, the reply was that he looked nicer.

But do you realise what I have done? I have described the same man. Mr Tidy is on his way to work. He has to look smart; it is part of his job. But at the weekend Mr Tidy doesn't bother to shave or wash, but he puts on some old

In God's law it says:

'Do not pervert justice; do not show partiality to the poor or favouritism to the great, but judge your neighbour fairly.'

Leviticus 19:15

Listen to what Peter says:

'I now realise how true it is that God does not show favouritism but accepts men from every nation who fear him and do what is right.'

Acts 10:34-35

clothes and boots because he's going out into the garden to do some work. So Mr Tidy has become Mr Scruffy.

So what do I mean by telling you all this? I am telling you that you must not form an opinion of other people simply by how they look. Mr Tidy is no more trustworthy than Mr Scruffy. The rich are not better than the poor. Those who shave in the morning are not necessarily nicer people than those who don't shave every morning. Just because you have shiny shoes does not mean that you love God more than someone whose shoes desperately need a clean. If I tell you the truth, I NEVER clean my shoes!

Samuel's mistake

So we must not judge people by their outward appearance, and then favour them above others. When Samuel was about to anoint one of Jesse's sons as king of Israel, he saw Eliab, who must have looked like a king, and thought, 'Surely the Lord's anointed stands here before the LORD.' But the LORD said to Samuel, 'Do not consider his appearance or his height, for I have rejected him. The LORD does not look at the things man looks at. Man looks at the outward appearance, but the LORD looks at the heart.' (1 Samuel 16:6-7). Even the great Samuel made that mistake. He saw that Eliab looked tall and strong, just like a king, and was about to favour him above his brothers, but he was wrong and God had to intervene.

Consider Jesus

Now I certainly don't mean to be rude when I say this, but it is probably true that Jesus looked more like Mr Scruffy than Mr Tidy. Jesus didn't have a nice new suit to wear, but he probably wore the same clothes for quite a while and maybe they got a bit grubby

and had a few holes in them. His sandals were dirty from walking the dusty roads. He often slept outside, so he probably didn't brush his hair every morning, and he had a beard so he didn't shave. In other words, he looked more like Mr Scruffy than Mr Tidy, but there is no one in this world who you can trust more than Jesus.

Let me put it this way. Jesus wore old clothes and yet he was a king and should have been wearing a crown and royal robes. He slept outside, but should have had the master bedroom in the royal palace. He was poor, with virtually no possessions to his name, and yet he is the Creator of the universe and all that is in it belongs to him. He was crucified as a common criminal, and yet he is the Saviour of the world. If you had known nothing about Jesus and had seen him hanging on the cross, what would you have thought of him? Would you have said, 'Look, there is the King of kings and Lord of lords, who upholds all things by his power'? Or would you have

said, 'Look, a poor criminal getting what he deserves'? How dangerous it is to judge people by their outward appearance.

What is the condition of your heart?

God is not really interested in what clothes you wear, whether or not you are following the latest fashions and styles, but he is interested in the condition of your heart. Do you love the Lord your God with all your heart? Is he more precious to you than anything else? Is he your all in all? Why don't you give Jesus your heart now, either for the first time or as an act of re-dedication?

> **Memory Verses**
>
> 'Do not judge others, or you too will be judged. For in the same way as you judge others, you will be judged, and with the measure you use, it will be measured to you.'
>
> **Matthew 7:1-2**

Time to think

1 Why is it wrong to judge others by their appearance?

2 Why is it wrong to show favouritism?

3 Is your heart right with God?

Time to pray

1 **Ask God to forgive you for judging others by their outward appearance.**

2 **Ask him to help you to love the rich and poor.**

3 **Pray for someone you know who is poor.**

Are you Rich in Faith?

JAMES 2:1-7

'Listen, my dear brothers: Has not God chosen those who are poor in the eyes of the world to be rich in faith and to inherit the kingdom he promised those who love him?'

What is faith?

'Now faith is being sure of what we hope for and certain of what we do not see.'

Hebrews 11:1

Now if you are rich, it means you have a lot of money. So if you are rich in faith it means you have a lot of faith. What exactly is faith? It is believing in and trusting in God as he is revealed in his Word. In other words, when the Bible tells us that God is love we believe it and feel confident in trusting our lives into his hands. When the Bible tells us that God is Almighty and that nothing is impossible for him, then we pray with assurance that he can do whatever we ask of him. When we read that God created the world in six days, we don't doubt it, but accept it without argument. When the Bible tells us that Jesus died for the sins of the world, then we know that if we repent and believe our sins will be forgiven.

A Bible promise

Besides that, the Bible promises that 'if we confess our sins, he is faithful and just and will forgive us our sins and purify us from all unrighteousness'. (1 John 1:9). So when we go to God and say sorry, he will forgive us because he keeps his Word, and faith believes that Word.

The stars in the sky

Think of Abram. He and his wife were both old and well past the age for having children. Abram was worried that a servant in his household would be his heir and not one of his own children, so he told God about how he was feeling. God took him outside into the night and said, 'Look up at the heavens and count the stars — if indeed you can count them. So shall your offspring be.' Have you ever gone out into a dark night and tried to count the stars? It's an impossible task. You start counting and get to about 243 and then you lose your place and have to start all over again. Or maybe you just realise that there are too many stars to count.

Abram's faith

Anyway, Abram, who had no children at that time, was told that his children were going to be as numerous as the stars in the sky. What was Abram's reaction? Did he start arguing with God, saying it was ridiculous for him to say such a thing? Did he remind God that he didn't even have one child? Did he point to his wife and explain to God that she was too old to have any children, naturally speaking? No, he didn't say any of these things. The Bible tells us his reaction: 'Abram believed the LORD, and he credited it to him as righteousness.' (Genesis 15:6). Abram believed the Lord. That's faith. That's being rich in faith, to take God at his Word, without questioning or doubting.

Blind Bartimaeus

Let me give you an example of rich faith from the New Testament. Blind Bartimaeus was sitting by the roadside begging. When he heard that Jesus of Nazareth was passing by, he began to shout out, 'Jesus, Son of David, have mercy on me!' Those nearby told him to be quiet,

> **Listen to what Joshua said when he was about to die:**
>
> 'You know with all your heart and soul that not one of all the good promises the LORD your God gave you has failed. Every promise has been fulfilled; not one has failed.'
>
> **Joshua 23:14**

but he shouted all the more, 'Son of David, have mercy on me!' He knew that if he could only attract Jesus' attention, he would be made well, and no one was going to put him off. Jesus called him over and Bartimaeus threw his cloak to one side and jumped to his feet.

Jesus asked him, 'What do you want me to do for you?'

'Rabbi, I want to see,' replied the blind man.

'Go,' said Jesus, 'your faith has healed you.' Immediately he received his sight and followed Jesus. (Mark 10:46-52).

True faith

True faith never gives up, and although others discouraged Bartimaeus, he was not going to stop shouting out to Jesus. He needed help and he was certain that Jesus would answer his cry.

Both Abram and the blind man were rich in faith. They both believed God when he spoke, they both trusted in his Word and so they both inherited the kingdom God has promised to those who love him.

True faith rests in God's promises. It is calm in the midst of a storm

because it has its eyes on Jesus. It knows God and trusts that he will provide all it needs.

A hungry dog

A famous preacher had a dog, which he used to feed at the dinner table until his wife objected. The dog seemed to sense why his food supply had dried up, so when the man's wife was not looking the dog crept under the table and rested his head on his master's knee, silently waiting. And sure enough, every now and then his master, who just couldn't resist the dog's silent pleas, and when his wife wasn't looking, cut up his food and secretly slipped some of it under the table to the grateful animal.

Faith waits on God

In many ways faith is like that. It rests on God and waits for him to provide us with what we need. It knows God loves us and will not let us down, so it looks up to him expectantly.

Are you rich in faith? Do you wait patiently for God to answer your prayers? Do you trust in his promises and believe his Word? Or do you grumble and fuss and fret? Do you try and work everything out in your own strength? Turn now from your doubts and unbelief. Ask God to forgive you and to make your faith stronger.

> **Memory Verse**
>
> 'And without faith it is impossible to please God, because anyone who comes to him must believe that he exists and that he rewards those who earnestly seek him.'
>
> **Hebrews 11:6**

Time to think

1 What is faith?

2 Why can't we please God without faith?

3 Is unbelief sin?

Time to pray

1 **Ask God to forgive you for doubting his Word.**

2 **Ask him to give you a much stronger faith.**

3 **Praise him that he will never let you down.**

'Love your Neighbour as Yourself'

JAMES 2:8-13

'If you really keep the royal law found in Scripture, "Love your neighbour as yourself," you are doing right. But if you show favouritism, you sin and are convicted by the law as law-breakers.'

In the Old Testament there are 613 laws. There are 365 laws that say 'Don't' and 248 laws that say 'Do'. In other words, God's law is not only negative in the sense that it tells us what not to do, but it is also positive in that it tells us what we should do. It is very interesting if you read through God's law because it is all about how we should love God and love our neighbour.

Be generous

If I just pick one law out at random, you will see what I mean.

Did you know?

'When you give to the needy, do not let your left hand know what your right hand is doing, so that your giving may be in secret. Then your Father, who sees what is done in secret, will reward you.'

Matthew 6:3-4

In Leviticus 19:9-10, it says, 'When you reap the harvest of your land, do not reap to the very edges of your field or gather the gleanings of your harvest. Do not go over your vineyard a second time or pick up the grapes that have fallen. Leave them for the poor and the alien [stranger].' What God is saying is look out for the poor, those less fortunate than you. Don't be greedy, but be kind and generous. Such commands are probably what you're told to do today at home and at school.

The Ten Commandments

In the Ten Commandments these 613 laws are reduced to 10. The first four are to do with our relationship of love with God, how we must treat him, respect him and worship him. And the next six are to do with our relationship of love with one another, how we are to treat and respect each other.

The most important commandment

One day Jesus was asked by one of the teachers of the law, 'Of all the commandments, which is the most important?'

Jesus answered, 'The most important one is this: "Hear, O Israel, the Lord our God, the Lord is one. Love the Lord your God with all your heart and with all your soul and with all your mind and with all your strength." The second is this: "Love your neighbour as yourself." There is no commandment greater than these.' (Mark 12:29-31). With these two commandments Jesus was summing up the Ten Commandments, or reducing them to just 2.

Love your neighbour

In our reading, James is further reducing the commandments to just one: 'Love your neighbour as yourself.' This is the Christian message. For if we love our neighbour in the way God wants us to, then we are also loving God. We cannot love our neighbour if we do not love God, and we cannot love God if we do not love our neighbour.

God is love

In the Bible it says over and over again that God is love. If there is one characteristic that is at the top of the list when it comes to describing God, it must be love. God is patient and kind. He does not boast. He is not rude or self-seeking. He is not easily angered. He does not delight in evil, but rejoices with the truth. He is love, perfect love, eternal love. Perhaps the greatest verse in the Bible is John 3:16: 'For God so loved the world that he gave his one and only Son, that whoever believes in him shall not perish but have eternal life.' We only have to look at the life of Jesus, who is God in the flesh, to see that God is love. He loves everyone and he has no favourites.

Do we love ourselves?

If we are to be like God, we must have no favourites and love our neighbour as ourselves. It is easy to love ourselves. We are always thinking about ourselves and looking after 'number one'. We feed ourselves, keep ourselves warm, spend money on ourselves, enjoy ourselves, protect ourselves and so on. Nobody has to tell us to love ourselves. But we do need to be reminded to love our neighbours. We must think about them and do all we can to help them. If they are hungry, we must feed them. If they are cold, we must give them clothes to keep warm. We must be kind and generous to them.

A kind orphan

I read about a little orphan boy who used to sell newspapers on the corner of the street. One day a man stopped to buy a paper from him. As he was searching for his money, he asked the boy where he lived. 'I live in a little cabin way down in the middle of the city, on the river bank.'

'Do you live on your own?' asked the man.

'Oh no,' replied the newspaper boy. 'I live with my friend Jim. He is a cripple and he can't work. He's my pal.'

Then the man said without thinking, 'You'd be better off without Jim, wouldn't you?'

'Oh no, sir,' said the boy, with a scowl on his face. 'I couldn't spare Jim. I wouldn't have anyone to go home to without Jim. And, mister, I wouldn't want to live and work without having someone to share with, would you?'

The boy's simple reply went to the man's heart and he was sorry for his thoughtless question.

We all need people to share with, not just to take from. We need others to care for and look after. If we only have ourselves to think about, our lives will be lonely and sad. So fulfil the whole law of God by loving your neighbour as yourself.

Memory Verses

'Dear friends, let us love one another, for love comes from God. Everyone who loves has been born of God and knows God. Whoever does not love does not know God, because God is love.'

1 John 4:7-8

Listen to John:

'This is how we know what love is: Jesus Christ laid down his life for us. And we ought to lay down our lives for our brothers. If anyone has material possessions and sees his brother in need but has no pity on him, how can the love of God be in him? Dear children, let us not love with words or tongue but with actions and in truth.'

1 John 3:16-17

Time to think

1 Who is your neighbour?

2 How can you love your neighbour?

3 What acts of kindness can you show the children in your class at school?

Time to pray

1 **Pray for three children in your class.**

2 **Pray for your brothers and sisters, or, if you are an only child, pray for your best friend.**

3 **Ask God to make you less selfish.**

Be Merciful

JAMES 2:8-13

'Speak and act as those who are going to be judged by the law that gives freedom, because judgement without mercy will be shown to anyone who has not been merciful. Mercy triumphs over judgement!'

We should live our lives knowing that God is watching every move we make, hearing every word we speak, understanding every thought we have, and seeing every attitude and desire we hold.

God sees

That means when we go off in a temper because we can't get our own way, or sulk because things haven't worked out in the way we had wanted, or we act unkindly towards someone at school, God sees. He is watching every time we get up in the morning and have our breakfast. Actually, someone has said that Jesus is the silent guest at every meal. He is watching our behaviour at school and how we treat others. Are we loving our neighbours as ourselves? He is watching how we conduct ourselves on the sports field and what we do at play times. He sees us as we journey home and what we do in the evenings. There is no time of day or night when God does not see us.

The long word 'omniscient' means that God hears and sees and knows everything.

God hears

It means that God hears very clearly what we say and how we say it. What do we say to our friends and how do we say it? Do we say nasty things behind other people's backs? How do we talk about our teachers and parents, with respect or do we make fun of them? Do we ever misuse the name of God or say rude things to others? Whatever we say and however we say it, whether we shout it from the rooftops, or whisper it under our breaths, God hears. And one day we shall be called to account for all we have said.

God knows

And what about our thoughts? The dangerous thing about thoughts is that we think they are secret. In one sense that is right. Unless we tell others our thoughts, they will never know them. But we must remember that God knows even our most personal thoughts. What we think about others is known to God – it is known by him as clearly as if we had shouted it out at the top of our voices. In many ways, it is frightening to think God knows our thoughts, because we have all thought some pretty awful things about others. If all our thoughts were suddenly revealed to the world, I expect we would want the ground to open up and swallow us, so ashamed would we feel.

Finally, our attitudes and desires. What is our attitude when we are asked to do something we don't like? What is our attitude towards those people we just don't like? Do we hold selfish desires? Do we always want to receive more praise than others, to get better marks in tests than our neighbours so we can silently congratulate ourselves?

Be merciful

The reason I have gone on about all this is because there are times when we need to examine ourselves in the light of God's Word. One day we shall all stand before God to give account of our lives, and one of the questions I can imagine him asking us is: Have we been merciful to others? In other words, have we forgiven all who have hurt us? Have we said things about them that are true and fair? Have we thought things that have helped us to love them? Has our chief desire been to glorify God in the way we have treated our neighbour?

The mercy of Jesus

One of the best examples of mercy in the Bible is when the teachers of the law and Pharisees brought to Jesus a woman who had been caught in adultery. Under the law a person convicted of such a sin was to be stoned to death. The teachers of the law and Pharisees asked Jesus for his opinion about what should be done to such a woman. Now it is clear that Jesus hated all such sin, but at first he said nothing, just wrote on the ground with his finger. But they kept questioning him, so he straightened up and said these never-to-be-forgotten words, 'If anyone of you is without sin, let him be the first to throw a stone at her.' Now Jesus was without sin, but what did he do? After everyone had left, he looked at the woman and asked, 'Woman, where are they? Has no one condemned you?'

'No one, sir,' she replied.

'Then neither do I condemn you,' Jesus declared. 'Go and leave your life of sin.'

I wonder what went through the woman's mind. Did she whisper under her breath, 'Thank you, God, for your mercy'? Perhaps she even went up to Jesus and gave him a hug.

Forgive others

We don't know what she said or did, but we do know she received mercy. Under the law she deserved to be punished, but Jesus let her off. That's how we should treat others. That's what it is to be merciful. There is a wonderful verse in 1 Peter 4:8: 'Above all, love each other deeply, because love covers over a multitude of sins.' Just as God forgives us, so we should forgive others, 'because judgement without mercy will be shown to anyone who has not been merciful. Mercy triumphs over judgement!'

Memory Verse

'Blessed are the merciful, for they will be shown mercy.'

Matthew 5:7

Time to think

1 What is mercy?

2 Why should we be merciful?

3 If God watches us all the time, how should we live our lives?

Time to pray

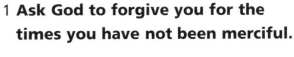

1 **Ask God to forgive you for the times you have not been merciful.**

2 **Ask him to help you love others.**

3 **Pray for someone you find hard to get on with.**

Faith and Deeds go Hand in Hand

JAMES 2:14-20

'What good is it, my brothers, if a man claims to have faith but has no deeds? Can such faith save him?...

'But someone will say, "You have faith; I have deeds."

'Show me your faith without deeds, and I will show you my faith by what I do. You believe that there is one God. Good! Even the demons believe that – and shudder.

'You foolish man, do you want evidence that faith without deeds is useless?'

It is very important to understand that faith and deeds in the Christian life go together. They are like the two hands of the Christian. With one hand we love God with all our heart and soul and mind and strength, and with the other hand we love our neighbours as ourselves. One without the other is, in the words of James, 'useless'.

Did you know?

'If I speak in the tongues of men and of angels, but have not love, I am only a resounding gong or a clanging symbol.'

1 Corinthians 13:1

Playing the guitar

Think of it this way. Have you ever played the guitar? With your left hand you finger the chords and with your right hand you strum or pluck. Now if you cut off your right hand and only fingered the chords with your left, you would not be able to make much of a sound - certainly not one that others would want to listen to. Or if you cut off your left hand and could only strum, I think the monotonous sound you would make would drive everyone mad!

A clanging symbol

So it is with the Christian life. If you say you love God, and yet show no interest in or concern for others, then you will not be able to make any beautiful music. Instead, your life will sound like a 'resounding gong or a clanging symbol', and who wants to listen to a noise like that? The apostle

John puts it strongly when he says, 'If anyone says, "I love God," yet hates his brother, he is a liar. For anyone who does not love his brother, whom he has seen, cannot love God, whom he has not seen.' (1 John 4:20).

A ridiculous thought

But what about the other way round? If you say you love others, but do not love God, you have again cut off one of your hands. It will be impossible for you to play tunes that will be attractive to the ear. You will be trying to love others in your own strength. If you succeed, others will congratulate you and you will receive all the praise. You will not be living for the glory of God. If the person you are trying to love becomes angry with you or rejects your love, you will be tempted to say, 'If that's all I get for trying to help you, you can sort things out yourself!' In times of difficulty, you withdraw your love. Besides, how can we be a Christian if we have no love for Christ? It's a ridiculous thought.

Faith and deeds

Faith and deeds must go together. What will happen to a train if you

A verse from the Old Testament:

'Hear, O Israel: The LORD our God, the LORD is one. Love the LORD your God with all your heart and with all your soul and with all your strength.'

Deuteronomy 6:4-5

take away one of the tracks? It will crash, of course! Can you tell the time correctly if you cut off the hour hand on your clock? Certainly not! How far will you be able to ride your bicycle if you unhook the back wheel? No distance at all. Faith without deeds is like digging up one of the tracks on which our lives move. It is like cutting off the hour hand, thus making even the most expensive clock in the world useless. It is like throwing away the back wheel of our bicycle, so that we can't do anything worthwhile for God.

It is worth mentioning that even the demons believe there is one God, and shudder at the thought, but they certainly have no good deeds to back up that belief.

Our perfect example

As always our example is the Lord Jesus Christ. Not only did he have perfect faith, but he had perfect love to support that faith. He had perfect love towards his heavenly Father and perfect love towards his

neighbour. He was always ready and willing to help others. He was never too busy or too tired. He never turned people away because he was in a bad mood or feeling selfish. Even when he was on the cross, at the height of his suffering, he responded to the dying thief who cried out to him.

Some serious questions

Can I ask you some serious questions about your Christian faith? It will be a good idea to answer each question before you read the next one. Do your classmates know you are a Christian? Do your teachers know you are a Christian? What was the last act of kindness you showed to your parents? If you have any brothers or sisters, do you look out for their interests as well as your own? Who was the last person you helped and in what way? Who was the last person to thank you because of your thoughtfulness?

Now I know these are difficult questions, but sometimes it's good

Memory Verses

'A new command I give you: Love one another. As I have loved you, so you must love one another. By this all men will know that you are my disciples, if you love one another.'

John 13:34-35

to examine ourselves to see if we are living lives that please God.

The best life in the world

Perhaps you're reading this and thinking, 'Well, I can't answer these questions because I am not a Christian.' If that's you, ask God by his grace to give you the gift of faith to believe in and follow him for the rest of your life, and to fill your heart with a sincere love for others. Being a Christian is the happiest and most rewarding life in this world.

Time to think

1 Why is faith without deeds useless?

2 What can you do to show Christian love to your classmates?

3 How did Jesus show his love for others?

Time to pray

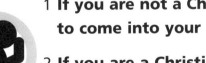

1 **If you are not a Christian, ask God to come into your life.**

2 **If you are a Christian, ask God to forgive you for selfishness.**

3 **Pray for someone you find hard to love.**

Consider Abraham

JAMES 2:20-26

'Was not our ancestor Abraham considered righteous for what he did when he offered his son Isaac on the altar?'

Listen to what Paul says:

'Consider Abraham: "He believed God, and it was credited to him as righteousness." Understand, then, that those who believe are children of Abraham.'

Galatians 3:6-7

I was tempted to deal with faith and deeds in just one chapter, but after thinking about it I realised that this whole area of 'deeds' is so important that it needs to be underlined. Sometimes we can be good at going to church and reading our Bibles and praying, but we forget to be a Good Samaritan to those around us.

Consider Abraham

James gives us two people to consider, one man and one woman. Let's deal with Abraham. When Abraham was seventy-five years old and childless, God promised to make him into a great nation. Now you can't become a great nation if you don't have any children. Some time later God said

to Abraham, 'I will make your offspring like the dust of the earth so that if anyone could count the dust, then your offspring could be counted.' (Genesis 13:16). Have you ever tried counting dust? An impossible task!

Counting the stars

God then took Abraham outside and said, 'Look up at the heavens and count the stars – if indeed you can count them. So shall your offspring be.' (Genesis 15:5). On a clear moonless night you can see a fuzzy band across the sky, which is part of the Milky Way. Maybe Abraham saw it when he looked up. The Milky Way is the galaxy in which we live. Do you realise there are about 100 000 million stars in

What amazing faith!

'By faith Abraham, when God tested him, offered Isaac as a sacrifice. He who had received the promises was about to sacrifice his one and only son, even though God had said to him, "It is through Isaac that your offspring will be reckoned." Abraham reasoned that God could raise the dead, and figuratively speaking, he did receive Isaac back from the dead.'

Hebrews 11:17-19

the Milky Way, which is about 200 stars for every person living on earth today? The galaxy is so big that it would take us about 100 000 years to travel from one side to the other. Blows your mind, doesn't it?

In other words, God was promising Abraham that he was going to have lots of children and grandchildren and great grand-children and so on. But at that moment he didn't have any. Was God playing games with him? No, God never tricks us.

'He laughs'
Eventually, when Abraham was 100 years old and his wife was 90, they had a son and they called him Isaac, which means ' he laughs'. And to be honest, it is funny to think of two very old people having children. Have you got an old granny? Or do you know someone very old? Can you imagine how people would react if she suddenly became pregnant? I expect there would be a few giggles.

Isaac, a burnt offering
After Isaac had been born and before Abraham had any more children, the Lord told him to take his only son, whom he loved, and to sacrifice him as a burnt offering. Now that must have been a shock to Abraham. Did he argue with God? Did he say, 'Lord, I'm afraid you must have made a mistake. Don't you remember your promises? How can I possibly sacrifice my only child?' No. He made no complaints. He didn't murmur under his breath. He didn't try to hide Isaac away.

What did he do? He got up early the next morning, took Isaac and some wood for the fire and set off in obedience to God's command. He was fully determined to kill his son. When he reached the place God had told him about, he built

an altar and arranged the wood on it. He bound Isaac and placed him on the altar on top of the wood. He then raised his knife to kill Isaac and at that point God stopped him. You can read the story in Genesis 22.

But what was Abraham thinking? We read in Hebrews 11:19 that Abraham thought that God was going to raise Isaac from the dead. You see, he trusted in God and he obeyed his Word. His faith and deeds were working together. His obedience was coming from his faith in God and his promises.

Believe and obey
Now the Bible is clear in telling us that every Christian is saved by grace through faith. But that faith must show itself in good deeds, it must show itself by actions that are pleasing to God. And how do we please God? By believing in him and obeying his Word.

So when we love our neighbours as ourselves, we are obeying the command of God and therefore pleasing him. When you are kind and thoughtful to your classmates, you are behaving in a way that God wants and supporting your faith with actions. When you treat your parents with respect you are putting into practice what you believe. If a girl falls over at playtime and you run over to help, and spend the rest of break sitting with her to comfort her, you are showing that girl that you believe in and love Jesus, the king of love. So put what you believe into practice. Love God, in whom you trust, and love others.

> **Memory Verse**
> 'And this is his command: to believe in the name of his Son, Jesus Christ, and to love one another as he commanded us.'
>
> **1 John 3:23**

Time to think

1 What do you call people who say they believe in God and then live bad lives?
2 Think of two ways to love your neighbour.
3 Why is it important to prove our faith by our deeds?

Time to pray

1 **Give thanks to God that his love is perfect.**
2 **Ask him to reveal his love for you more and more.**
3 **Ask him to help you to be good at school and at home.**

19 A World of Evil

JAMES 3:1-6

'The tongue also is a fire, a world of evil among the parts of the body. It corrupts the whole person, sets the whole course of his life on fire, and is itself set on fire by hell.'

Here is an important proverb: 'The tongue has the power of life and death, and those who love it will eat its fruit.'

Proverbs 18:21

Did you notice the strong words that James uses to describe the tongue: boasts, fire, a world of evil, corrupts and hell? Let's take just two of these words. Firstly, the word fire. Think of a forest fire. They have these kinds of fires in southern California or in the south of France. Before we went on holiday to France last year, we heard that there were huge fires very near where we were going to camp and that some sites had been closed. We called up our campsite to see if they were still open and they were, but they said they could see the smoke from the fires, which were 25km away.

Forest fires

These forest fires leave nothing but destruction in their path. After they have passed through an area, there is a black smouldering lifeless landscape. All the beautiful flowers and trees have been destroyed; all the animals have either died or run away to safety; maybe houses have been gutted and there is nothing left of a family's home except an empty shell. Fire destroys.

Rotten apples

Then take the word corrupt, which can mean rotten. In our garden we have an apple tree and every year beautiful apples grow on it, but almost without fail the wind blows them to the ground and I fail to pick them up. What happens to them? Slowly but surely they turn brown and become all mushy. Maggots start to live inside them, and by the time I get to them they are only fit to be thrown straight in the bin. You might eat a freshly picked apple from the tree, but I'm sure you wouldn't eat a brown, smelly, worm-infested apple that has been lying on the ground for a few weeks.

The tongue

In using words like fire and corrupt James is describing the tongue. Oh, he's not describing the slimy thing we love wiggling about, but the words that come out of our mouths. They are like fire and they corrupt, not only ourselves, but the people who are listening to us. Just as a fire destroys, so our tongues can destroy. We can corrupt others by leading them astray or by the foul language we use or the lies we tell about others. We can hurt and make our neighbours angry by the words we speak. That's why James said earlier in his letter that we are to be slow to speak. Clap your hand over your mouth, so those evil words do not come out.

The awful thing is that we can never take our words back. Once they have come out of our mouths, we can't chase after them and stop them from entering the ears of the person we are speaking to. No. It's then too late, and sometimes we deeply regret what we have said. So what should we do? Should we cut off our tongues?

Mrs Fusspot should read this proverb:

'He who guards his lips guards his life, but he who speaks rashly will come to ruin.'

Proverbs 13:3

Mrs Fusspot

I once read a story about a preacher, who was continually criticised by a member of his congregation. This woman was always saying personal and hurtful things about him. She complained about what he said, and how he said it; what he wore and what he didn't wear – he just couldn't win, for whatever he did was wrong. Now when he preached this preacher wore a gown and bands, which is a collar with two hanging strips either side (a bit like a long scarf). One day, Mrs Fusspot we'll call her, came up to him and said, 'Do you know, the bands that hang around your neck when you preach are much too long and they annoy me enormously. I can't stand it when you move your hands and it

catches your bands and they flick out sideways.'

'I'm very sorry,' said the preacher. 'I'll try hard not to move next time I preach.'

'I'm sure you won't mind if I cut them and make them shorter,' grunted Mrs Fusspot.

'No,' said the preacher graciously, and to his surprise Mrs Fusspot got out a pair of scissors and started to cut off the ends of the bands. After she had finished, the preacher, who by this time couldn't take any more, said, 'Now, Mrs Fusspot, there is something about you that is much too long, and I'm sure you won't mind if I cut it off.'

'Not at all,' replied Mrs Fusspot, handing him the pair of scissors and wondering what it was that was too long.

'Please stick out your tongue!' said the preacher with obvious delight.

Now I'm sure he didn't cut off her tongue, but he made the point. We don't have to cut off our tongues, but we often need to hold them tightly to stop them from saying hurtful words. There is a proverb, which says, 'However sharp is the knife, sharper yet is the human tongue.'

Remember the words of James

So remember the words James uses to describe the tongue and ask God to help you speak words that will help and heal and not hurt and destroy. 'Consider what a great forest is set on fire by a small spark,' and take note that friendships can be ended, enemies multiplied and wars started by the words we speak.

Memory Verse
'Whoever would love life and see good days must keep his tongue from evil and his lips from deceitful speech.'

1 Peter 3:10

Time to think

1 Why can words cause so much damage?

2 Who in the Bible got into trouble because of what he said?

3 What unkind words have others said to you?

Time to pray

1 **Thank God that all his words are faithful and true.**

2 **Ask him to forgive you for the hurtful things you have said.**

3 **Ask him to help you to think before you speak.**

20 Praise and Curse

JAMES 3:7-12

'With the tongue we praise our Lord and Father, and with it we curse men, who have been made in God's likeness. Out of the same mouth come praise and cursing. My brothers, this should not be.'

Once again James uses some very strong words to describe the tongue: no one can tame it; it is a restless evil and a deadly poison.

Circus animals

I don't know whether or not you have been to a circus, but some years ago they used to have many wild animals that would perform tricks during the show. Elephants would walk on three legs, and stand on their back legs with their trunks held high in the air. They would lift men up with their trunks and rest their huge feet on a man's chest without injuring him. Then the lion tamer would appear, with several ferocious lions in the large cage with him. The lions would obey his every command and the audience would watch spellbound, hoping the lions would not turn on their master.

?? Question ??
Can you think why it is so difficult to tame the tongue?

Man has tamed other animals such as bears, monkeys, birds of prey and dolphins, but nobody has yet managed to tame the tongue. It

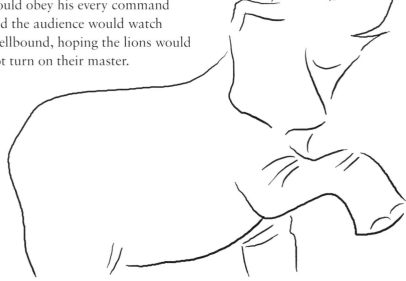

says what it wants when it wants, and it will pounce on anyone who tries to stop it. It is indeed a restless evil that is always looking for a victim, and a deadly poison that will quickly make a coffin for the person it attacks.

Just think for a moment about some of the nasty things you have said. Have you ever lost your temper and told someone you love that you hate him? I heard someone once tell their young child, who was annoying them, to go and play in the road, meaning go and get run over by a car. I was shocked when I heard it.

From praising to cursing

But what I want to concentrate on today is how easily we can go from praising God to cursing others and from cursing others to praising God. It's a bit like when you are having a flaming row with someone and shouting horrible things at them and the telephone rings. You pick it up and almost miraculously you become all sweetness and light, and it is as if butter wouldn't melt in your mouth as you greet in such a friendly manner the person on the other end of the phone.

Horrible words

Many years ago when I was living in California, I used to send taped messages home to my family to let them know that all was well. Once I was driving down the freeway with a tape recorder on my lap. I was speaking into it and letting my family know a little about the scenery. I then decided I would pray for them, so with my eyes open I started to pray. About halfway through my prayer a driver on the freeway swerved right in front of me and I muttered something unpleasant under my breath and then carried on with my prayer. I didn't think anything more of it until I listened to the tape recording before I sent it home. And I am so glad I did, because to my horror, in the middle of my prayer, those horrible words I had muttered were clearly audible. I had to scrub the prayer and start again. I also felt terrible as those words of James came into my mind: 'With the tongue we praise our Lord and Father, and with it we curse men, who have been made in God's likeness.'

A fire

If we go back to what we were saying last time about the tongue being a fire, we will also know that a fire, when it's controlled and in the right place, can make us warm and snug. There's nothing nicer than to curl up by a log fire during a cold evening. But if that fire was under our bed, it would not make us feel warm and snug! Certainly not! We would be out of that bed as fast as we could move, and it wouldn't matter if the evening was freezing.

For good and evil

You see our words can be used for good and evil, for praising and cursing, for building up and knocking down. In one breath we can be telling God how wonderful he is, and in the next breath we can be swearing at our neighbour. One moment we can be exalting Jesus for opening heaven's door, the next moment we can be telling our brother to go to hell. This should not be. It is unnatural for the Christian. It is as if the sea was made up of fresh water and the rivers of salt water. Imagine planting an apple tree and then picking oranges from it. It is not natural. And so to praise God and curse others is not right or natural for someone who has been born again.

I read a little poem the other day that makes the point about our words being used for good or evil.

A careless word may kindle strife,
A cruel word may wreck a life.
A bitter word may hate instil,
A brutal word may hurt and kill.

A gracious word may smooth the way,
A happy word may light the day.
A timely word may lessen stress,
A loving word may heal and bless.

If you are a Christian, then follow the advice of Paul: 'Do not let any unwholesome words come out of your mouths, but only what is helpful for building others up according to their needs, that it may benefit those who listen. And do not grieve the Holy Spirit of God.' (Ephesians 4:29-30).

This is what David says:

'I said, "I will watch my ways and keep my tongue from sin; I will put a muzzle on my mouth as long as the wicked are in my presence."'

Psalm 39:1

Memory Verse

'May the words of my mouth and the meditation of my heart be pleasing in your sight, O LORD, my Rock and my Redeemer.'

Psalm 19:14

Time to think

1 What does James mean when he calls the tongue a 'deadly poison'?

2 Why is it unnatural for a Christian to praise God and curse his neighbour?

3 When are you most likely to say hurtful things?

Time to pray

1 **Praise God for his goodness towards you.**

2 **Thank God for Jesus.**

3 **Ask him to help you speak wholesome words.**

'Who is wise and understanding among you? Let him show it by his good life, by deeds done in the humility that comes from wisdom. But if you harbour bitter envy and selfish ambition in your hearts, do not boast about it or deny the truth. Such "wisdom" does not come down from heaven but is earthly, unspiritual, of the devil.'

Wisdom is all about the way we live our lives and not about how intelligent we might be. In fact, James says there are two types of wisdom: good and bad. Let's look at good wisdom.

Good wisdom

Good wisdom is called heavenly wisdom because it comes from God. It is characterised by a good life, and

Look what Paul said to the Corinthians:

'I gave you milk, not solid food, for you were not ready for it. Indeed, you are still not ready. You are still worldly. For since there is jealousy and quarrelling among you, are you not worldly?'

1 Corinthians 3:2-3

by humility. James gives a list of the kind of things that make up this heavenly wisdom. It is 'first of all pure; then peace-loving, considerate, submissive, full of mercy and good fruit, impartial and sincere'.

Wisdom is peace-loving

Let's look at one of these things. Wisdom is peace-loving. I wonder how many arguments you have had recently. Think of your last argument, if you can remember it. Who was it with? What was it about? Who started it? Who ended it? It's always interesting to look at how an argument starts and how it ends. Usually you will find that arguments children have start because one of them does not get his or her own way. The boy in the back row wants something, but does not get it and as a result takes out his frustration on the girl sitting next to him. In other words, arguments are caused by selfishness. For an argument to end, someone has to give in. Either you admit you are wrong and say sorry or you simply stop answering back. If

an argument does not end, it usually gets worse.

Take revenge?

Recently at school we were talking about bullying and how children should respond if they are being bullied. Some of the children gave sensible answers, such as: tell someone, keep out of the bully's way, don't believe the nasty things the bully says, and so on. Then one girl shot up her hand and cried out, 'I know what we should do, sir, take revenge!' As you can imagine most of the class thought that was an excellent idea and burst out laughing!

Now imagine if everyone took revenge. You stick your tongue out at me, so I stick my tongue out at you. You call me an unkind name, so I call you one back. You push me, I push you. You kick me in the shin, so I kick you in the shin. You pull my hair, so I pull your hair. Unless one of us stops, where will it end? In a full-scale war, I expect. One of us has to be a peacemaker.

One of us has to call the other over and say, 'Listen, we are being very silly. Let's make up and become friends.' Now whoever makes peace is wise. He is loving peace more than war. By his life he is exercising heavenly wisdom.

The greatest peacemaker

Jesus said, 'Blessed are the peacemakers, for they will be called the sons of God.' (Matthew 5:9). Jesus, of course, is the greatest peacemaker. He came from heaven to this world to make peace between God and man. If you are not a Christian, you are not at peace with God. Your unbelief proves that you are God's enemy. You are on the opposite side to him. You are, as it were,

outside God's house, and on the front door are the words: KEEP OUT! Your sin has built up a wall of hostility between you and God and there is nothing you can do to break it down. In short, you are at war with God.

But Jesus came and died on the cross to make peace between sinful people and a holy God. When you become a Christian, you become God's friend. God takes down the KEEP OUT! sign on his front door, and exchanges it with one that says, WELCOME. He smashes down the wall of hostility that stood between you and him, and receives you with open arms. You are now his child and he is your Father. Instead of war, there is

peace. And this is all possible because Jesus, the prince of peace, died on the cross for sinners. He suffered the punishment that we deserve to make us right with God.

Are you like Jesus?

Are you like Jesus? What I mean is: Do you make war or peace with your school mates? Are you a troublemaker or a peacemaker? Do you start a fire or try to put one out? If you are a troublemaker, you are showing earthly, unspiritual wisdom that is of the devil. If you are a peacemaker, your wisdom comes from heaven and you are acting like Jesus.

Here is some good advice:

'Make every effort to live in peace with all men and to be holy; without holiness no one will see the Lord.'

Hebrews 12:14

Time to think

1 Why did Jesus die on the cross?

2 Why is it important not to take revenge?

3 What should you do if you argue with someone?

Time to pray

1 **Thank God for sending Jesus to die on the cross.**

2 **Ask God to forgive you for arguing.**

3 **Ask him to make you into a peacemaker.**

22 Friendship with the World

JAMES 4:1-6

> 'Don't you know that friendship with the world is hatred towards God? Anyone who chooses to be a friend of the world becomes an enemy of God.'

What exactly is friendship with the world? To put it very simply, it is to want our own way instead of God's way. It's to fight and quarrel so that we get what we want. It's to put ourselves first. It's to live for our own pleasures and not for the glory of God.

The bee in a pot of honey

Have you ever read about the bee that one day found a pot of honey? He flew down and sat on the edge of the pot, staring at the sweet-smelling honey. He said to himself, 'Now, if I jump in, I can eat as much as I want, and I won't have to keep flying around the fields looking for flowers. It will save me time and hard work, and besides, I shall really enjoy the lovely taste.'

So he leant over the side and started to lick the sticky honey. Slowly but surely he leant further and further over until he slipped right into the honey. At first he thought it was wonderful, so much honey, but after a while he started to feel tired and a bit sick, and he noticed that his wings were covered in honey. He tried to flap them but they were glued to his body and very heavy. He tried to move his feet but they were stuck in the

!! Warning !!

'But mark this: There will be terrible times in the last days. People will be lovers of themselves, lovers of money … lovers of pleasure rather than lovers of God — having a form of godliness but denying its power. Have nothing to do with them.'

2 Timothy 3:1-5

honey. He was trapped in all that sweet-smelling honey. And there he died, surrounded by pleasure.

A honey pot of pleasure

To be a friend of the world is to jump into a honey pot of pleasure, where we try and satisfy our selfish desires. It is to fight with those people who will not give in to us. It is to quarrel with those who stand in the way of our lusts. It is to covet the things of this world. It is to pray selfish prayers, expecting God to give us all that we want. To be a friend of the world means we do not give in to God, but we obey the desires that battle within us.

'Not my will'

When Jesus was in the Garden of Gethsemane, only hours away from his crucifixion, he prayed an amazing prayer: ' Abba, Father, everything is possible for you. Take this cup from me. Yet not what I will, but what you will.' (Mark 14:36). Jesus was wanting his Father's will before his own, which is the complete opposite of being a friend of the world. Although he was about to suffer the most terrible of deaths, he wanted to do what his Father wanted and not to follow his own desire.

The Bible is very strong on this point. To be a friend of the world is to show hatred towards God. It is to be his enemy. In other words, we cannot say we are a Christian, and then want our own way. To love God is to love what he wants. To follow Jesus is to deny ourselves and go God's way.

What have we learned?

During our study of James we have been looking at some very important subjects. We have been told to keep our tempers, to listen to God's Word, to love our neighbours, to practise what we preach, to hold our tongues, to live wisely and not to be selfish. If we

are honest, we fail at all these things. We get very angry, sometimes with little provocation. We get distracted when listening to God's Word. We certainly don't love our neighbours as ourselves. We might occasionally say what is right but we often do what is wrong. We speak without thinking and say some pretty hurtful things. We sometimes cause trouble at school and at home, and more often than not we are selfish in our desires and actions. It can be a bit discouraging at times.

We need a Saviour

One thing all of this shows us is how much we need a Saviour. We can never get right with God by our own efforts, because we do so

many things wrong. It's as if God is at the top of the longest ladder in the world, but we can't even climb onto the first rung because of all our sin. Or he is hiding behind a huge wall that is 1000 miles high and 1000 miles thick and all we can do is scratch away at it with our bare hands.

But the wonderful news of the gospel is that when we give our lives to Jesus he carries us up that ladder right into the arms of God. He lifts us over that wall and places us in the kingdom of God. Yes, we fail miserably, but Jesus has succeeded. We cannot do anything to earn salvation, but Jesus has opened the door to heaven to all who believe. We were drowning in our sin, but Jesus is our life belt. We were trapped in a burning house, but Jesus has put out the flames. We were groping around in darkness, but Jesus has turned on the light. In every sense he is our Saviour.

Turn to Jesus

So even if you are a friend of the world, there is hope for you if you turn to Jesus. He can make you a

friend of God. He can turn your hatred towards God into a deep and real love for him. He can change your selfishness into a desire to serve God with all your strength. He can take all your horrible sins and throw them away once and for all.

So turn to Jesus now. Give him your whole life. Hold nothing back. Tell him how sorry you are for all the things you have done wrong in word, thought and deed. Ask him to make you clean and to carry you up that ladder to God. Ask him to rescue you from the punishment you deserve and to make you one of his followers.

Time to think

1 What is it to be a friend of the world?

2 What's wrong with selfishness?

3 Why is Jesus our Saviour?

Time to pray

1 **Ask God to forgive you for all you have done wrong.**

2 **Give your whole life to him.**

3 **Ask God to help you tell others about Jesus.**

Submit, Resist, Repent

JAMES 4:7-12

'Submit yourselves, then, to God. Resist the devil, and he will flee from you. Come near to God and he will come near to you. Wash your hands, you sinners, and purify your hearts, you double-minded. Grieve, mourn and wail. Change your laughter to mourning and your joy to gloom. Humble yourselves before the Lord, and he will lift you up.'

There are three important words that come from today's reading: submit, resist, repent. Let's deal with them in reverse order.

Repent

The first word then is **repent**. Notice the word is not penance, but repent. There is a big difference. A minister once found some children reading the Douay version of the New Testament, and he saw that the word repent had been translated 'do penance'. So he asked the children what was the difference between the words penance and repent. A short silence followed as the children thought hard for an answer. Then a little girl put up her hand and said, 'I know, sir. Judas Iscariot, after he betrayed Jesus, did penance when he went out and hanged himself. Peter, after he had denied Jesus three times, repented when he wept bitterly over his sin.'

That little girl was quite right. Penance is when you punish yourself for your sin. Repentance is when you accept the punishment that Christ suffered for you. Penance will not receive God's forgiveness, because you are trying to earn it by punishing yourself. Repentance will receive forgiveness because you are receiving the gift that God has promised to all who repent and believe.

The important thing about repentance is that we are truly sorry for what we have done wrong. Sometimes it is easy to *say* sorry without *being* sorry for what we have done. True repentance is when we *say* sorry and *feel* sorry for what we have done. True repentance makes us ashamed of what we have done and determined not to do it again. We bow our heads and hardly dare to look up to heaven, yet all the while the precious blood of Christ is washing us.

Resist

The second word is **resist**. That means we do not do what the devil wants. If the devil whispers in our ear that we should lie to our

Watch out!

'Be self-controlled and alert. Your enemy the devil prowls around like a roaring lion looking for someone to devour. Resist him, standing firm in the faith.'

1 Peter 5:8-9

teacher in order to escape a punishment, we say a firm no to him. If our friends tempt us to go shoplifting with them, we say a firm no to them. If we have the chance to cheat in an exam because our neighbour does not cover over his answers, we refuse to look across. In everything, we are to be like Jesus, who when he was tempted by the devil in the desert said a firm no to him every time.

Submit

The third word is **submit**. That means we do what God wants. We obey his Word, even if it means we get into trouble for it. We obey his Word even if others tell us not to. After Peter and John had healed a crippled beggar, they were commanded by the authorities not to speak to the people in the name of Jesus. But they boldly replied, 'Judge for yourselves whether it is right in God's sight to obey you rather than God. For we cannot help speaking about what we have seen and heard.' (Acts 4:19-20). A little later the apostles were arrested and put in jail. After an angel of the Lord had set them free, they were again arrested. This time they said, 'We must obey God rather than men!' (Acts 5:29).

A little girl
There will be times in our lives when we will have to obey God

rather than men. If your teacher told you to steal, you would have to disobey her. If your parents told you to lie, you would have to disobey them. There was once a little girl, who lived next to a school. During the holidays a preacher was going to the school to conduct a series of gospel meetings. The girl's dad hated Jesus and everything to do with Christianity and he would not allow her to go to the meetings. The girl really wanted to go and hear about Jesus, but she did not want to disobey her dad. During

the first meeting she heard them singing next door, and she really felt as if the Lord was telling her to go to the meeting. She did not know what to do. Should she obey her dad, or should she obey the Lord?

During the second meeting she listened to the singing until she felt she had to go. So she quietly crept downstairs and out of the front door and into the meeting. It was a little while before her dad discovered that she was not in the house. He immediately marched into the school in a rage. He flung open the door and saw everyone on their knees praying to God. He stormed up to his daughter, grabbed hold of her and was about to charge out of the room, when she turned to him, and, with such a look of peace and love on her face, said, 'It's too late, daddy, I have given my heart to Jesus.'

These simple words deeply affected him, and he could not resist the love of God any longer. He fell on his knees and there in the

schoolroom cried out to God to have mercy on his soul. Very soon he found the Saviour, whom he had tried so hard to shut out of his own heart and that of his daughter's.

This little girl's obedience to Jesus brought about a wonderful change in the life of her family.

What to do every day
In many ways our daily walk with Jesus can be summed up in these three words: repent, resist and submit. Submit to God and his Word every day. Resist the temptations of the devil every day. Repent of all sins every day.

Time to think

1 What does the word submit mean?

2 Who should we resist and why?

3 What does it mean to repent?

Time to pray

1 **Ask God to help you obey his Word every day of your life.**

2 **Ask him to strengthen you against the devil's temptations.**

3 **Say sorry to God for all the things you have done wrong.**

Do not Slander

JAMES 4:7-12

'Brothers, do not slander one another.'

What is slander? It is to say something unkind or untrue about someone else, especially when they are not around. It is to criticise or blame them for wrongdoing behind their back. It is to find fault and judge others by our own standards. When we say slanderous things, we do not love our neighbour as ourselves.

At school

I remember when I was a boy at school, talking to some of my friends. During the conversation I left the room and I had a sneaky feeling that they were going to talk about me. So I did something really foolish. I left the door slightly open and listened at the door. Sure enough, before very long, they started to talk about me, and what I heard was not very pleasant. I felt hurt and angry that one minute they could be so nice to me, and the next they could say horrible things about me.

If we are honest, we have all said unkind things about others behind their backs. We have all joined in with gossip and made comments that are either not true or unfair about others. We have not made correct judgements.

Judge fairly

Think of a judge in a court of law. He first of all listens carefully to both sides of the argument, considers the facts, thinks long and hard about what he hears, and then makes a decision according to the law that is absolutely fair. A slanderer, on the other hand, usually only listens to one side of the argument, ignores the facts, does not think carefully about what is said, and makes judgements that are unfair. That's why it is not right in the sight of God to speak against our Christian brothers or sisters.

We also have to be very careful about listening to what others say about people we know. Gossip can separate close friends. If we pay attention to stories that might not be true, it can cause us to criticise others unnecessarily.

A big 'news bag'

I read a story recently about a good woman called Jane Parsons, who was keen to live at peace with everyone, especially with those who lived near her. But there was a neighbour called Agnes Saundry, who was such a 'news bag', and was always going to Jane's house

What should we do?

'Get rid of all bitterness, rage and anger, brawling and slander, along with every form of malice. Be kind and compassionate to one another, forgiving each other, just as in Christ God forgave you.'

Ephesians 4:31-32

?? Question ??

Why do we find it so easy to say nasty things about other people?

to share with her the latest 'story'. Once Agnes started talking she would just go on and on, and Jane found it very hard to stop her. She never really knew how much of what Agnes told her was true, and how much of it was made up.

Jane found these one-way conversations difficult and

she saw all the aeroplanes she guessed it was somewhere abroad, but she still had no idea where. She thought it might be Guernsey, where we spent our honeymoon. When we arrived at the airport I gave her a little present. She opened it and it was a book on Lisbon. 'We're going to Lisbon!' she exclaimed, and gave me a big hug. The thrill of the surprise was written all over her face. After the weekend I asked her which she would have preferred: being told a few weeks before our trip, or the surprise. Without hesitation she said the surprise. So surprises are great fun and part of the fun of life.

In all this I'm not saying we should not plan for the future, but I am saying we should thank God that we don't know the future. We certainly should not boast about the future. All our boasting should be in the Lord.

Death is certain

The second thing we know for certain is that we are going to die. James says our life is like a mist. What happens to a mist when the sun rises in the morning? It disappears. Our life is like that. We are here one day and gone the next. We are like a candle flickering in the wind. At any moment our life can be blown out.

A few years ago my cousin got up and went to work at his bank. He had a slight headache that morning, but thought nothing of it. Lots of people get slight headaches. Halfway through the day he was violently sick and fell into a coma. He was rushed to hospital, where he died three days later. A day that had begun like any other, ended in tragedy. One day we are all going to face death.

God holds the future

In view of what I have said, we need to know that God holds the future. We may not know what is going to happen, but God does. He knows the beginning from the end. He has planned each day for us and has promised to look after us. Never forget that he loves us and our lives and deaths are in his almighty hands. His grace is sufficient and we can trust him for all things. He is faithful and true and will never let us down. So we mustn't worry about the future, but submit to our Saviour. If happy times are ahead, let us get ready to praise him and thank him for his goodness and love towards us. If sad times are ahead, let's get ready to trust him come what may and to live our lives for his glory. He is a big strong God who will hold our hands all the way to heaven.

Do you know this hymn?

'Because he lives I can face tomorrow; because he lives all fear is gone; because I know he holds the future, and life is worth the living just because he lives.'

Time to think

1 Are you thankful you do not know the future?

2 What surprises have you had recently?

3 Why shouldn't a Christian be afraid of the future?

Time to pray

1 **Thank God that he holds the future in his hands.**

2 **Ask God to help you not to worry about the future.**

3 **Pray that he would help you live for him always.**

26

Rich and Selfish

JAMES 5:1-6

'Now listen, you rich people, weep and wail because of the misery that is coming upon you.'

Jesus said:

'No one can serve two masters. Either he will hate the one and love the other, or he will be devoted to the one and despise the other. You cannot serve both God and Money.'

Matthew 6:24

Did you notice the strong language that James uses to describe what's going to happen to these rich and selfish people? He is telling them to weep and wail because of the misery that is coming upon them. All the wealth they have so carefully collected has rotted like an apple and moths have eaten their expensive clothes. Their silver and gold have rusted over and become useless. Their flesh, so often covered in rich oils and creams, will burn away. The Almighty God is against them because of their selfishness and greed. All they have done as they have lived in luxury is to fatten themselves ready for the day of slaughter. Now, if that doesn't put you off living for money and being selfish with it, I don't know what will.

Dying of thirst

I read a story about a man who was terrified of dying of thirst. He lived on a farm and everyday he collected as much water as he could find and poured it into a pond he had made. He cut little trenches in the ground so that whenever it rained all the water would run in the direction of the pond. He set up barrels all around his farm so they would catch the rainwater as it rolled off the roofs of his buildings. He then carried the barrels and emptied them into the pond. He even restricted the amount of water his animals could drink. Any puddle he found he tried to scoop up the water and take it to his pond. When the pond was full he felt relaxed and happy, but when the water was getting low he started to panic and could not sleep at night because he was worrying so much. One day, as he was carrying a barrel of water, he slipped and fell into the pond and drowned.

Do you love money?

'Poor man,' you say. 'All his life he had been frightened of dying because of too little water, and in the end he died because of too much water.' Yes, it's a sad story, but isn't it true of many people today who are trying so hard to get rich? They spend so long every day thinking of ways to make money. All they do is for one end only, and that is to save as much money as possible so they can retire early and then live a life of selfish pleasure. They put out their barrels, as it were, to collect all the money they can. They never give any away because they want it all for themselves. They cheat others and pay them as little as possible. All they are doing is fattening themselves for the day of slaughter. One day they will drown in all that money they have so carefully hoarded. It will burn them up and destroy them, and, unless they repent, send them to a lost eternity.

Money drowns God

The trouble with the love of money is that it blinds us to the truth and hardens our hearts against God. We become so eager to get more money that we no longer want to do what God says. We ignore his Word. We are only interested in becoming rich and buying all the things we dream of. We don't live for God's glory, we live for money and pleasure and the things money can buy. In other words, money drowns God in our lives.

That's why Jesus said it is easier for a camel to go through the eye of a needle, than for a rich man to enter the kingdom of heaven. Now it's impossible for a camel to squeeze through the tiny eye of a needle. And so it is impossible for a rich man to enter heaven, unless he turns away from his greed and selfishness and seeks first God's righteousness.

It is worth remembering that we can never buy our way into heaven. We can never pay for salvation or give God a bribe to forgive us. Salvation is a free gift and it is a huge insult to God if we try to pay for it.

Store up treasures in heaven

Instead of thinking about ourselves, which the love of money forces us to do, we should be thinking about God and how we can live a life that pleases him. The Christian life is not about storing up possessions here on earth, where moth and rust destroy and thieves break in and steal. No, it is about storing up treasures in heaven, where nothing can destroy and no thief can steal. We should be more determined to serve God than to serve ourselves.

Think of Jesus

So my reader, don't be selfish and mean, be generous. If you are ever tempted to be selfish, just think of Jesus. He gave up his palace to be born in a stable. He gave up his home in glory to live in this sinful world. He gave up all the riches of heaven to live as a poor man. He gave up the joy of paradise to become a man of sorrows. He gave his time and energy to help others. He gave up his life to save bad people from hell. He didn't have to leave heaven. He could have stayed with his Father, but he was willing to give his all so that people like you and me could go to heaven.

Live for Jesus

Make sure the desires of your heart are right. Don't crave money, but earnestly desire to know Jesus. Don't live your life to get rich, live your life to serve Jesus. Don't live for yourself, live for Jesus. Why live for money? You are only fattening yourself for the day of slaughter. Live for Jesus and he will prepare for you a home in heaven. Live for yourself and you will spend eternity in hell. Live for Jesus and you will never regret it.

Time to think

1 Why is it wrong to love money?

2 Why is it wrong to be selfish?

3 Do you find it easy to share?

Time to pray

1 Thank God for Jesus and his death on the cross.

2 Ask God to forgive you for being selfish.

3 Ask him to help you to be generous.

27 Be Patient

JAMES 5:7-12

'Be patient, then, brothers, until the Lord's coming. See how the farmer waits for the land to yield its valuable crop and how patient he is for the autumn and spring rains. You too, be patient and stand firm, because the Lord's coming is near. Don't grumble against each other, brothers, or you will be judged. The Judge is standing at the door!'

It's hard to be patient sometimes. We all like things NOW! Our society is an 'instant' society, which means we are not used to waiting. Everything is given to us so quickly. But sometimes we have to wait, perhaps for an exam result at school, or a letter or parcel to arrive in the post, or for our birthday.

Caught in an earthquake

Sometimes it's good to wait, especially if we have an important decision to make, or we are waiting for an injury to heal before we start playing games again. I remember hearing about a man who was caught in an earthquake in the middle of the night. He was walking along the street when he was thrown to the ground by the violent shaking. All the lights went out and he found himself in the middle of the road. He didn't know what to do. Should he get up and try to find his way home, or should he just wait where he was until morning when he could see where he was going? He decided to

What does David say?

'Wait for the LORD; be strong and take heart and wait for the LORD.'

Psalm 27:14

wait patiently for the sun to rise. When the sun finally rose he was amazed at what he saw. The earthquake had ripped open the road just in front of him. If he had decided to walk home in the dark, he would have fallen to his death. Yes, it's good to be patient.

Do you ever grumble?

The trouble is that when we feel impatient we tend to grumble and blame others. We criticise them and judge them, although it might not be their fault. I don't know whether or not your mum and dad, when they are in a hurry to get

somewhere, grumble about the other drivers on the road. Do you grumble if your brother or sister is taking ages to get ready in the morning and you are in a hurry to go out? What are you like if you are really hungry and your mum is taking a long time to make the meal?

God rules

When we feel impatient and start grumbling, we are in no mood to thank God for his goodness and mercy towards us and to be content with what he has provided. If we are impatient for something to happen, we are really blaming God for not bringing it to pass earlier. God's timing is perfect. He never makes a mistake and he is in control of all things. So even when things appear to go wrong, take comfort in the fact that God rules all things and will accomplish his purposes.

Think of the disciples

Think of the disciples. How frightened and confused they were when Jesus was crucified. They could not understand what was going on. The one in whom they had placed all their hope was hanging on a cross. Their king and Saviour was dying like a common criminal. The Romans were executing the man who had performed so many miracles and had spoken the words of eternal life to them. They thought Jesus was going to set them free from the Romans and here they were killing him. So they locked themselves in a room, confused, frightened and without hope.

If only they had known that all they had to do was wait – just three days. In three days all their dreams would again be alive. In three days their king and Saviour

would open heaven's door. In three days they would know that Jesus had overcome the devil and all demons, sin, the world and hell. In three days darkness would turn to

light, fear would be replaced by joy and despair with hope. In three days all their questions would be answered and the storm that was raging in their souls stilled.

Don't panic

So if you are going through a hard time, wait on the Lord. Lift your fears and difficulties into his hands. Cast your anxieties on him because he cares for you. Don't panic for he has everything under control. Wait patiently for his timing and trust him that he will bring his purposes to pass.

The farmer waits patiently

Consider the farmer who plants his crops and then waits. He trusts that the autumn and spring rains will arrive on time and that miraculously the seeds he planted will begin to grow. He doesn't rush out into his fields every morning to see if there is any sign of growth and start panicking when he sees nothing.

No, he knows it will happen. And he waits patiently. Then at harvest time he gathers the crops into barns and later sells them.

God is never in a hurry

You must be like the farmer and patiently wait for God to move in his own way in his own time. God is never in a hurry. He has all the time in the world. So instead of panicking and grumbling, thank God that he has everything under control. Look in the Bible and remind yourself how faithfully God worked in the past. Look back in your own life and see how God turned difficult situations around for good. Trust in him with all your heart and lean not on your own understanding; in all your ways acknowledge him, and he will make your paths straight.

> **Memory Verse**
> 'Be joyful in hope, patient in affliction, faithful in prayer.'
>
> **Romans 12:12**

Are you doing what God says?

'Humble yourselves, therefore, under God's mighty hand, that he may lift you up in due time. Cast all your anxiety on him because he cares for you.'

1 Peter 5:6-7

Time to think

1 Why do we grumble when we feel impatient?

2 Can you think of a bad situation in the Bible that God turned to good?

3 Who in the Bible was very patient?

Time to pray

1 Thank God for all that he has given you.

2 Ask him to help you trust him every day.

3 Pray for someone you know who is finding life difficult.

28 Patience in Suffering

JAMES 5:7-12

'Brothers, as an example of patience in the face of suffering, take the prophets who spoke in the name of the Lord. As you know, we consider blessed those who have persevered. You have heard of Job's perseverance and have seen what the Lord finally brought about. The Lord is full of compassion and mercy.'

James just loves giving examples to back up what he is saying. He turns immediately to the Old Testament prophets and urges his readers to consider them in their Christian fight. Look at Elijah for example and how desperately Ahab tried to kill him. Spurred on by his wicked wife Jezebel, he did his utmost to put Elijah to death.

Look at Daniel

Or what about Daniel? How would you like to be thrown into a den of hungry lions? Imagine sitting there with the lions prowling around you. At first they might not know what to do as they stare at you, licking their lips and thinking about the tasty meal they are about to enjoy. Gradually they creep nearer and nearer and start to roar. You sit there without moving a muscle, all the time praying as hard as you can. Just as the lions are about to pounce an invisible hand seems to hold them back. They try to open their mouths but cannot. They stare at you but they cannot touch you. God has come to your rescue. Praise fills your soul as you thank God for his power and mercy.

Both Elijah and Daniel experienced many difficulties in life, but neither of them gave up following God and obeying his Word. They suffered, but they also waited patiently for God to act on their behalf. They were not disappointed.

Think about the sufferings of Job

Think about poor Job. Is there anyone that you know who has suffered more than Job? He was a blameless and upright man in the sight of God. One day a messenger ran up to Job and told him that his oxen and donkeys had been stolen and some of his servants killed. While he was still speaking a second servant arrived and exclaimed to Job that fire had fallen from heaven and burned up his sheep and servants. While the second servant was still speaking a third messenger arrived and told Job that his camels had been stolen and more of his servants killed. While the third messenger was still speaking yet another messenger came and told Job that while his sons and daughters were feasting and drinking wine at the oldest brother's house, a mighty wind had swept in from the desert and struck the house. It collapsed on them and killed them all.

What was Job's reaction to this terrible news? Did he blame God? Did he refuse to obey God because he had not stopped these terrible things from happening? No.

> ### After God had rescued Daniel, King Darius wrote:
> 'For he is the living God and he endures for ever; his kingdom will not be destroyed, his dominion will never end. He rescues and he saves; he performs signs and wonders in the heavens and on the earth. He has rescued Daniel from the power of the lions.'
>
> **Daniel 6:26-27**

Instead, he tore his robe and shaved his head as a sign of deep mourning. Then he fell to the ground in worship and cried, 'Naked I came from my mother's womb, and naked I shall depart. The LORD gave and the LORD has taken away; may the name of the LORD be praised.' (Job 1:20). In all that Job said, he did not sin by charging God with wrongdoing.

But this wasn't the end of his suffering. Some time later he was afflicted with painful sores from the soles of his feet to the top of his head. They were so sore that he took a piece of broken pottery and scraped himself with it as he sat among ashes. And though his wife tried to get him to curse God and die, he refused. He did not sin in what he said.

The blessings of Job

This was a terrible time of suffering for Job, but he did not give up his faith in God. He persevered. And in the end God blessed him by giving him twice as much as he had before. All his brothers and sisters, and everyone who had known him before, came and ate with him in his house. They all comforted him and brought him a piece of silver and a gold ring. The Bible then says that God 'blessed the latter part of Job's life more than the first. He had fourteen thousand sheep, six thousand camels, a thousand yoke of oxen and a thousand donkeys. And he also had seven sons and three daughters.' (Job 42:12-13).

God loves us

We see clearly from these examples that the Lord is 'full of compassion and mercy'. He is not hard and uncaring. He loves us and is always ready to hear our cry for help. When we are in trouble he wants to rescue us and to bless us as never before. We only have to look at the life and ministry of Jesus to see what God is like. Many of Jesus' miracles were performed because he had compassion on those who were hurting and in need. We read that his heart went out to them, that he was moved to heal them.

So remember next time you are in trouble, that God is a loving God, who cares for his children. He is a Father who protects his children from danger. He is like a mother who picks them up when they fall and comforts them when they are distressed. He is a Good Shepherd, who tenderly carries the sick and hurting in his arms. He is a king who fights on their behalf and provides them with all they need.

A wonderful verse:

'He tends his flock like a shepherd: He gathers the lambs in his arms and carries them close to his heart; he gently leads those that have young.'

Isaiah 40:11

He is the Saviour who rescues them from their enemies.

Never give up

Just as God never gives up on us, so we must never give up on him. He has never promised his children they will never suffer, but he has promised to be with them forever and to bring them safely to his heavenly kingdom. I hope you will never have to suffer like Job, but I hope you will always have his determination to be faithful to God. If you are faithful to God through a time of suffering, he will bless you afterwards more than you can imagine.

Memory Verse

'Be still before the LORD and wait patiently for him; do not fret when men succeed in their ways, when they carry out their wicked schemes.'

Psalm 37:7

Time to think

1 Who else in the Old Testament suffered a great deal?
2 Why does God take us through times of suffering?
3 What is important to remember when you are suffering?

Time to pray

1 **Ask God to reveal more of his love to you.**
2 **Ask him to help you persevere through times of suffering.**
3 **Pray for a member of your family who is not a Christian.**

29 You must Pray

JAMES 5:13-20

'Is any one of you in trouble? He should pray. Is anyone happy? Let him sing songs of praise.'

Prayer for the Christian is like breathing. It is absolutely vital. If we do not breathe, we are not alive. If we do not pray, we are not a Christian. It is as simple as that. A Christian *must* talk to God, *wants* to talk to God and *needs* to talk to God. He realises how important it is to pray and to talk to God about everything. If he is in trouble, he asks God to help him and to give him strength. If he is happy, he sings praises to God and gives him thanks for his goodness. If he is sick, he asks others to pray for him. If he sins, he goes to God and says sorry for all the wrong things he has done.

The power of prayer
A Christian knows the power of prayer. Elijah, an ordinary man, prayed earnestly that it would not rain and the Lord heard and answered his prayer; it did not rain on the land for three and a half years. After that time he prayed that it would rain and once more the Lord heard his prayer; the heavens gave rain and the earth produced its crops.

Unable to speak
There was once a man who did not believe in God and he was going to a certain city to give a lecture about his unbelief. He was a great speaker, who could hold huge crowds spellbound by what he said. It was feared by the Christians in that place that his lecture would cause considerable spiritual harm among the young people. So they agreed to pray fervently together that God would in some way hinder the meeting.

The evening of the meeting arrived and the man stepped onto the platform before a huge audience, who were eagerly waiting to hear what he had to say. Some of the Christians were in the crowd and they were still praying hard that God would intervene and stop him from speaking. After a few introductory remarks by the chairman, the unbeliever stepped forward and began to speak. 'Ladies and gentlemen,' he began. Suddenly he paused and wiped his brow with his hand. 'Ladies and gentlemen,' he said for a second

time. Again he paused. There was a long silence, which was eventually broken by the words, 'Ladies and gentlemen.' Again the man stopped, and seemed to be in some distress. He turned to the chairman and said, 'For some unknown reason, sir, my mind is all mixed up and clouded. I am unable to speak. I am very sorry to disappoint the audience.' He then sat down. The chairman apologized to the crowd, who slowly but surely left the hall, wondering what had happened. Of course the Christians knew and were filled with thanksgiving to God for answering their prayers. The man never returned to that city.

We must pray because prayer is powerful and effective. The reason prayer is powerful and effective is because God is powerful and listens to the prayers of his children.

Pray for yourself

In our reading James is saying that we should *pray for ourselves*. If we are in trouble, we must ask God to come and help us. If we are worried, we must ask God to fill our hearts and minds with peace. If we are afraid, we must ask God to give us courage. If we are sad, we must ask God to comfort us. If we are confused about what to do, we must ask God to make the way ahead plain to us. If we are ill, we must ask God to heal us. If we are tempted, we must ask God for the strength to say no and to live a holy life. If we sin, we must ask God to forgive us for Christ's sake. And so I could go on. In other words, we must pray for ourselves in every situation in which we find ourselves. There is never a reason not to pray for ourselves.

Ask others to pray for you

James is also saying that we should *ask others to pray for us*. We must never be ashamed or embarrassed of asking someone else to pray for us because we are finding things tough. If you are sick, ask the elders of your church to pray for your healing. If you are being bullied at school, ask your friends to pray that the Lord would stop the bully from hurting you. If

you are finding it difficult to resist temptation in a certain area, ask your mum and dad to pray that God would make you strong enough to say no. If you are finding it hard to be kind to others, share it with a Christian friend and ask her to pray that the Lord would soften your heart and give you a real love for others. Keep asking others to pray for you, so that you might become a better follower of Jesus.

Pray for others

James is also telling us to *pray for others*. If your dad is finding it hard at work, pray that the Lord would help him to overcome the problems. If your sister is unhappy at school, pray that the Lord would comfort her and provide her with all she needs to be content. If there are children in your class who are not Christians, pray that God would open their eyes to the truth and they would see Jesus, the wonderful Saviour. If your next door neighbour is experiencing difficulties, pray that he would turn to the Lord and cry out for his help. Pray for your pastor, pray

for your enemies, pray for your teachers, pray for your relatives.

I called this chapter 'You must Pray' and that is what I want to encourage you to do. Pray always. Pray without ceasing. Be devoted to prayer. Pray day and night. Never stop praying. I think you've got the message. Jesus is a wonderful Saviour and he hears all our prayers.

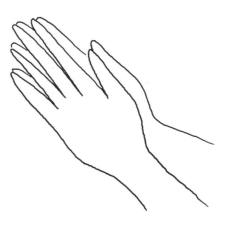

Follow this advice:

'Do not be anxious about anything, but in everything, by prayer and petition, with thanksgiving, present your requests to God.'

Philippians 4:6

Time to think

1 Why is prayer so important?

2 What should we pray about?

3 How often do you pray?

Time to pray

1 **Pray for yourself.**

2 **Pray for a member of your family.**

3 **Pray for someone at school.**

30 Keep on Keeping on

JAMES 1:2-8, 12, 22-25; 2:8-11

'Blessed is the man who perseveres under trial... Do not merely listen to the word, and so deceive yourselves. Do what it says... If you really keep the royal law found in Scripture, "Love your neighbour as yourself," you are doing right.'

As we end these series of readings I would like to remind you of three very important things that we have been looking at. They are really the foundation to everything else. Our Christian lives must be built on these three foundation stones or else we will get into serious trouble.

Keep following Jesus

The first is *keep following Jesus*. Don't let anything or anyone put you off. If your friends laugh at you, ignore them. If your teachers tell you that your beliefs are silly or old fashioned, run to Jesus for help. Keep on keeping on. Besides, if you don't follow Jesus, who are you going to follow? Remember what Joshua told the people of God. He said, 'If serving the LORD seems undesirable to you, then choose for yourselves this day whom you will serve... As for me and my household, we will serve the LORD.' (Joshua 24:15). So who are you going to follow? Jesus, the King of Kings and Lord of lords, who holds all power and authority in his hands, or are you going to serve yourself or some pop star or the devil?

Only Jesus

Is there anyone other than Jesus who can forgive your sins and prepare you for heaven? Has anyone else promised never to leave or forsake you? Jesus is your Saviour, who rescues you from hell. He is your light and he delivers you from darkness. He is your friend and he will never be unfaithful to you. If you follow someone else, what will your future hold? You will be led into darkness to serve a cruel master, who will eventually lead you into the unquenchable fire.

So never give up following Jesus. Give him your whole life every day. Remember, we looked at the word persevere. If you persevere in your faith you will become mature and

!! Warning !!

'Jesus replied, "No one who puts his hand to the plough and looks back is fit for service in the kingdom of God."'

Luke 9:62

complete, not lacking anything. You will receive the crown of life that God has promised to those who love him. If you follow Jesus, love and life and glory will be yours. So keep on keeping on.

Keep obeying God's Word

The second foundation stone is *keep obeying his Word*. If you listen to God's Word and then do not obey it, you trick yourself into thinking you are a Christian. Faith without deeds is useless. If you listen to God's Word and do not put it into practice, you are like a man, who looks at himself in a mirror and, after looking at himself, goes away and immediately forgets what he looks like. You are like the foolish man who built his house on the sand. When the rains came, and the streams rose and the winds beat against his house, it fell with a great crash.

If God tells you to do something, do it, without arguing or complaining. When you read the Word, ask God to help you obey it. Don't let it go in one ear and out the other. Submit to it. Let it be the rule of your life. Let it point you in the right direction, that is, away from wrongdoing and towards Jesus. If you obey the Word of God, it will protect you from all sorts of dangers. It will warn you of the dangers of sin and tell you how to live in order to please God. Sin may give you a moment's pleasure; it then bites like a poisonous snake. Sin may sometimes look attractive, but its pathway leads to death. It may wave and smile at you as it tries to entice you, but in the end it will cut your throat and throw you out into the street. The Bible warns you of these dangers and points you in the opposite direction.

The Day of Judgement

God's Word may be hard to obey sometimes, especially if your friends do not want to obey it. But keep on keeping on. One day they will have to stand before God and give account of their lives, just as you will. If you have been faithful in obeying his Word, he will be pleased with you and you will hear those wonderful words, 'Well done, good and faithful servant! You have been faithful with a few things; I will put you in charge of many things. Come and share your master's happiness!' (Matthew 25:21). Your friends, on the other hand, who didn't want to obey God, will be thrown outside, into the darkness, where there will be weeping and gnashing of teeth. So keep on keeping on.

Keep loving your neighbour

The third foundation stone is *keep loving your neighbour*. That's also hard to do sometimes, especially if you find them difficult and they make fun of you because of your faith. But Jesus told us to love our enemies and to pray for those who are horrible to us. When Jesus was on the cross, he looked at the people who were saying cruel things about him and the soldiers who had crucified him and he prayed, 'Father, forgive them, for they do not know what they are doing.' (Luke 23:34).

So if you ignore the needy and say to the naked and hungry, 'Go, I wish you well; keep warm and well fed,' but do nothing to help them, you do not love your neighbour as yourself. If you show favouritism to the rich by always offering them the best seats, while you say to the poor sit on the floor by my feet, you do not love your neighbour. If you fight and quarrel because you cannot have your own way or because someone else gets what you want, you do not love your neighbour.

Instead, comfort the sad and stand with the lonely. Talk to that girl in your class who no else talks to.

Share with others and never be mean. Pray for the boy you sit next to who finds most of the work difficult and always gets low scores. Always be kind to others and ready to share your faith with them.

Keep on keeping on

In all these areas, keep on keeping on. Then you'll find that your life will be happy and fulfilled. As you draw near to Jesus, he will draw near to you. As you obey his Word, he will bless you more than you can imagine. As you love your neighbour, you will experience the love of God in an ever-increasing way.

Time to think

1 How do we follow Jesus?
2 In what areas of your life are you not obeying God's Word?
3 How do you treat the other children at school?

Time to pray

1 Ask God to keep you close to Jesus all your life.
2 Ask him to help you obey his Word every day.
3 Ask him to increase your love for others.

Notes

Notes